A Summer Wedding In The Highlands

Alexandra Wholey

Copyright

ISBN (Paperback) 978-1-7395877-5-8

ISBN (Ebook) 978-1-7395877-4-1

Dedication

For my Family, with love always xx

Glossary

Aye Yes

Baltic. Very cold (usually winter related)

Bairns Children

Blethering Bickering

Braw Good/ Really good

Cannae Can't

Ceilidh Traditional Scottish party with music and dancing.

Clype. A gossip/ Tell tale

Couldnae. Couldn't

Craic Enjoyable social activity, a good time.

Didnae. Didn't

Dinnae. Don't

Doesnae. Doesn't

Dreich. Rainy dull weather

Hadnae. Hadn't

Hasnae. Hasn't

Havenae. Haven't

Hen. Term of endearment towards a lady

Isnae. Is not/ Isn't

Och. Oh! An exclamation of expression

Shouldnae shouldn't

Shouldae Should have

Sleekit. Sly, cunning

Stoating. It's stoating down, rain falling so hard it bounces off the ground.

Stooshie. To bicker or have a quarrel

Stramash. To have a full blown argument.

Wasnae Wasn't

Weans. Another term for Children

Willnae Will Not

Whisht   To shush someone

Wouldnae Wouldn't

Content Warning

This page is the page for you if you want to know what potentially difficult content you might encounter in this book. This may contain SPOILERS which hint at plot lines (or even briefly moments in the story.)

Death of relative (grandmother, off page) discussed and mentioned on page, grief over this loss, and coping with this grief is a main theme in the story.

Diagnosis of terminal cancer for secondary character, and discussion on page of this in detail.

Death of relative (mother,) discussed and mentioned on page, grief over this loss, and coping with this grief is a main theme in the story.

On page discussion of ectopic pregnancy of secondary character resulting in baby loss (before 12 weeks) and coping with this loss is a theme in the story.

A Summer Wedding In The Highlands

Alexandra Wholey

Prologue

*T*he Past.

Winter.

At Cairnmhor Farm, in Mossbrae in the Inner Hebrides, the scent of lamb stew filled the kitchen as eight year old Grace Kincaid balanced precariously on the stool next to her mother, Annabelle, as she collected the ingredients for the honey cakes they were having for pudding.

"Are we all ready?" Joe, her father asked from the doorway and Grace turned to see her younger brother, Angus, seven, and sister, Robyn, who was almost five, pulling on their wellies and coats ahead of this morning's gather. The gather was the gathering and bringing of the sheep from the hill in preparation for getting them scanned for how many lambs they were having later in the season. The Kincaids had run their home, Cairnmhor Farm, in the quaint little village of Mossbrae, in the Inner Hebrides, for almost four generations, and ran a herd of two hundred pure bred Scottish Blackface Ewes. The sheep lived up on the hillside the majority of the year, only brought down for lambing checks, shearing, and if the winter storms were too wild in this part of the Inner Hebrides.

Turning her attention to the wintery weather outside, Grace shuddered. "Can I stay here with you? I want to do baking."

"Och, hen, you said you were gonnae help Da with the sheep," Annabelle replied gently. "We can bake when you come back."

"But it's so cold, and it's gonnae snow!"

Annabelle gently ruffled her dark hair which was fastened into a ponytail, admiring how much she looked like Joe with her dark hair and blue eyes.

"Come on, Gracie!" Angus called, wiping the toast crumbs from his chin as he pulled on his coat.

"Aye, come on!" Robyn called, heading to the door, and grabbing Joe's hand. "We're waiting!"

Grace reluctantly got down from the stool and headed towards the front door as Annabelle watched her with a warm smile.

"I know you want to stay with Ma," Joe said as he helped her own with her coat and wellies. "But I really need all your help."

Grace turned to him now. "Really?"

"Aye, of course. Do you know why?"

She shook her head.

"Why?" Grace whispered back.

"You are the best whistler," Joe said in a conspiratorial whisper.

"Really?" Her eyes widened with surprise.

"Aye. All the sheep come running when you whistle for them. It'll take us no time at all to get them in, and the sooner we get the sheep in, the sooner you can come back, and bake with Ma. We'll have those honey cakes for pudding, aye?"

"So would you like to come and give me a hand?"

She nodded, glancing back at Annabelle, a small smile creeping across her face.

"That's my girl…" Joe said proudly, and whistled for their sheep dogs, Rum, Whisky, and the pup, Betty, who came rushing to the door, ready to go and work.

they all headed outside into the wintery morning.

"Bye, Ma!" Grace called as she bid goodbye to Annabelle and followed them out of the door, Robyn already kicking the snow, blonde fluffy hair bouncing around her face, looking like their mother's mini me.

"Dinnae forget your hat!" Annabelle called. "Have a grand time!"

For Grace, the gather turned out to be fun as she sat on the back of her little child's quad, alongside Angus on his, and wee Robyn with Joe, watching the dogs as they expertly brought the sheep in, thanks to Joe's expert commands and Grace's whistles.

"Da!" Robyn called as they headed home a couple of hours later. "I wanna be a sheep doctor."

"You mean a vet," Grace said expertly.

"Aye?" Joe asked. "That's a grand job. What about you, Angus?"

"A shepherd," Angus replied.

"Gracie?"

"Guess!" Grace replied.

"No' a farmer?" Angus asked in surprise.

"Or a vet?" Robyn asked. "Whit about the lambs? I love lambs! I'm gonnae help Da when they all come. I love the lambing shed!"

"Urgh!" Gracie cried, flinging her hands over her mouth in disgust. "The smell makes me feel sick!"

"Och, you dinnae have to worry about that just now," Joe reassured her. "What do you want to be?"

"A baker. I want to own a bakery," Grace said dreamily, looking out at their hill farm, eyes shining with excitement, as they headed back to the farm. "I'm gonnae own my own bakery when I'm grown up…"

∼

Present Day.

Winter. Burns Night.

. . .

The delighted whooping and cheering filled the dance floor of The Dog and Duck, as the lively opening notes of the Dashing White Sergeant struck up as the Burn's Night Supper got underway. With the crackling roaring of the log fire, and the happy atmosphere, no-one was thinking about the wintery weather. With the delicious buffet Grace Wallace had provided, everyone was distracted, not thinking about the week long storm which had wrecked havoc, icy weather, the blizzards, or the fact the ferries were not currently running.

Everyone had made it tonight, Grace Wallace noted as she took in the room, recognising all the familiar faces: The Trinity (Enid, Nelly and Maudie, her godmothers), Nigel, her brother Angus and his fiancee, Eilidh, her younger sister Robyn and her husband Orion, and Paul, her husband, who was dancing with their kids, Mhairi and Ollie. Even Rory, her cousin, had made it all the way from the Highlands with his wife, Isla and baby William, who had just turned one. He had been born here in Mossbrae, in the middle of a blizzard, and it had been Eilidh and Angus who had delivered him.

"Och, Grace, this is braw!" Maudie's voice broke into her thoughts as sighed in pleasure as she took another spoonful of the raspberry Cranachan Grace had made especially for the occasion. Her pink hair bounced around her shoulders as she chuckled.

"Thank you," she replied, her face cracking into a broad grin, her own dark hair loose around her shoulders. She was wearing a peridot green shirt dress, and her eyes sparkled with pure happiness.

"I cannae believe you're gonnae be interviewed for Visit Scotland!" Maudie continued, candy floss pink hair bouncing around her shoulders. "Congratulations! I'm so pleased for you, hen!"

"Thank you, it's been a long time coming!" Grace agreed, as she took another rare sip of whisky.

"You'll have to put your skills to the test soon enough," intoned Enid, making one of her premonitions. "There's a wedding to plan."

"Eilidh and Angus need encouraging!" Maudie added, smiling over at them across the dance floor now, who were linking arms and laughing as they spun each other around.

"I should hope so!" Grace replied hopefully. "They said they were gonnae start planning the wedding soon, but you know what those two are like, twenty odd years and they've only just got together!"

Nelly nodded and tutted loudly. "About time they bit the bullet!"

"They need us to show them how a Highland wedding is really done."

"Aye, that's right!" Maudie agreed, blowing as kiss over to Nigel as she danced with Grace now. "We know how to plan a braw wedding, don't we, lass?"

"Aye," Grace replied, recalling her own wedding to her husband Paul, and how wonderful it had been.

"Especially after all the trouble poor wee Eilidh had last time with that ex-fiance. The one who ran off with his ex-girlfriend."

"It made way for Angus to confess his feelings at last, though," Grace added, and Enid nodded solemnly. "He wasnae the one for her. Angus is the one for her. That's plain to see. I knew it, all those years afore."

"I know a seamstress!" Nelly affirmed, and Grace nodded in agreement, feeling emotion well up in her throat as she admired them now. If anyone deserved their happy ending, it was those two...

"Jeannie Christie," Enid intoned. "She's the best in the Highlands..."

Nelly nodded enthusiastically. "But where to hold it?"

"What's this?" Rory called as he and Isla danced over to them.

"We're planning a wedding. Their wedding!" Grace laughed. "We're wondering where they could hold it."

"They can have it our place," Rory replied amiably. He owned a Georgian mansion on a sixty acre estate. "We have a license for weddings."

"Och, that's a wonderful idea!" Grace cried, and Maudie nodded.

"We're gonnae show them how we do a wedding, and one to remember. It'll be the Wedding of the Year!"

7

TOP 5 PLACES TO VISIT IN SCOTLAND FOR LOCAL FOOD EXPERIENCES

30th March 2023

Looking for a special food experience when on holiday? Want to head out and about and sample local delicacies? Here are just a few of the top places to visit for an unforgettable local food experience.

1. Four Ducks Bakery, Mossbrae, Inner Hebrides.

Post by @graceatfourducksbakery

Owned and run by Grace Wallace at Four Ducks Bakery in the quaint little village of Mossbrae, Four Ducks Bakery has recently opened in March, specialising in locally sourced honey cakes and custom made celebration cakes. Cakes can be made to order and delivered, as well as collected in person. Grace, who also lives at Cairnmhor Farm, runs the farm shop which is responsible for selling home bred lamb and venison, as well as home produced honey which she uses for the honey cakes.

View Grace's most recent updates via her instagram page @graceatfourducksbakery for more information.

This month we have been interviewing local businesses in and around Scotland, and this week it is the turn of Four Ducks Bakery, run by Grace Wallace, mum of two, whose dreams of running a bakery from childhood became a reality earlier this year. Let's dive in.

Hello Grace, how are you doing this morning?
Hello! It's lovely to be here.

Congratulations on opening your new bakery! What started your love of baking?
I grew up on a sheep farm, where I currently live with my husband and kids, called Cairnmhor Farm. We ran Blackface sheep and I would help with the sheep during the week, and I used to bake with my mother on weekends. We made pies, and cakes, and I knew from then, I wanted to be a baker. I went to catering college and honed my skills from there. My family have always been very supportive on me wanting a career in something other than farming.

What do your siblings do? Are they in farming? Do you have a close relationship?
My younger brother, Angus runs the farm now with my husband, and my younger sister is a vet, but we all live locally and see each other all the time.

When you first saw Four Ducks Bakery, how did you know it was The One for you and how long did it take you to renovate?

Me and my husband Paul first saw it at auction over the summer. The bakery used to be an old sweet shop, and it reminded me of the old sweet shop in a Roald Dahl story. In all, it took us six months to renovate. We decorated, and installed the ovens, which were delayed due to the winter storms.

What is the best thing about living your dream?

I get to do the thing I've always dreamt of every day. I love the whole process of cake making, the mixing, the icing. My favourite bit is the icing part. And now my kids are growing up, they like to join me at weekends and after school, and my daughter also loves baking.

What's the worst thing?

I think the weather makes it a little unpredictable, especially in winter, as we get a lot of storms here in the Inner Hebrides. This means the ferries stop running, and it means the tourists can't make it across from the mainland.

There has been a surge in tourism in Mossbrae over the next few years. How much do you rely on the tourist industry as a small business and how does it help or hinder business?

Like many small businesses we rely a lot on

tourism. It helps boost our popularity, as I locally source a lot of the ingredients I use in my baking. I use a variety of honey sourced from my brother's fiancee's hives. She and my brother run the branch of our farm's honey business, Cairnmhor Farm. I would say the only way tourism hinders the business is when the weather is unpredictable and we don't get the influx of tourists we tend to do in the warmer months.

What's your ultimate goal for Four Ducks in the future? Keep the business afloat. I'm hoping Four Ducks Bakery will be around in five years time, and will become a household name. I love it when I get calls from potential customers who tell me they've heard about the bakery and can't wait to check us out.

What's next for Four Ducks Bakery? What's your next goal?

I'm completing the ultimate bake, I'm going to make my best friend's wedding cake. She and my brother are getting married this summer, and I'm hoping it'll be the best cake of my career.

Ooh! That sounds wonderful. Any spoilers?

I can't give any spoilers at the moment. But I'll be sure to get some photos of it for Instagram.

So, to wrap up, how can potential customers get hold of you and keep in touch with you?

We're on social media. We have an Instagram page.

It's @graceatfourducksbakery, and I post on there regularly. We also have a website with all the contact details on there, it's The Four Ducks Bakery. Com.

WEDDING INVITATION

Eilidh

&

Angus

27th June 2023

CAPERCAILLIE, FOCHABERS, THE SCOTTISH HIGHLANDS

Chapter One

 resent Day

Summer had finally come to Mossbrae, the quaint village in the Inner Hebrides. It was a gloriously warm May Day, and the honey season was well under way, and Angus and Eilidh's wedding was in three weeks time.

"Ma! *Ma!*"

Grace winced at the sound of her five year old daughter, Mhairi dragging the stool across the stone kitchen of their farmhouse at Cairnmhor Farm.

"Aye? Ollie, have you fed the ducks afore we go? Mhairi, come on now, we need to get to Uncle Angus and Aunty Eilidh's. You and Ollie have your wedding outfit fittings, and your beekeeping lesson."

Eilidh, who lived down the road at Honeybee Cottage, had been a beekeeper since childhood and had recently begun giving Mhairi and Ollie beekeeping lessons.

. . .

She turned to Ollie now, who, nodded as he obediently pulled his coat on. Their pet Runner Ducks, Strawberry, Apple, Custard, and Jelly, lived on the farm and were kept for eggs which they sold at the farm shop alongside all the rest of the produce they made on the farm. "Good, lad."

"Can we make honey cakes?" Mhairi interrupted.

"Och, Mhairi, we cannae do it now. We havenae got any honey. I'm gonnae have to get some from Aunty Eilidh."

Mhairi gave a whoop of excitement and rushed towards the front door. "Bye, Grandad! See you later!"

"We'll no' be long, Da," Grace assured her elderly father, Joe, who was finishing his toast and tea in the living room.

"Och, dinnae fret," Joe replied, waving a hand. "I'll be fine for five minutes. You're only off away down the lane. Just be back in time for us heading for the kilt fitting."

"Aye, well, just so you know," Grace replied.

"He'll be fine," Paul, her husband reassured her.

"His heart…" Grace murmured, as she pulled on her coat. "He's no' getting any younger…"

Joe had had to have emergency heart surgery two years ago, following a heart attack and a history of heart problems. In order to take care of him, Grace, Paul, and their kids had moved back to the farm, to live with him. Luckily, Joe had recovered quickly, but it meant retiring fully from working on the farm. Angus had taken over, running the farm with Paul, who had given up a job in I.T. to help Angus.

"Gracie, it's been almost two years. He's fine. He's taken his daily meds, is that no' right, Joe?" Paul turned to Joe now, who nodded assuringly. "See? Angus and Dougie are outside."

Dougie, son of family friend, Jim Sinclair, had had recently, joined the fold six weeks ago, to help out with lambing when the time came. He was in his early twenties, lean and wiry and was a great farmhand, and Angus and Paul were relieved to have someone else on hand when they were so busy. Dougie was a good one, and he had even agreed to watch the farm whilst everyone was away for the wedding. Everyone liked him, especially the dogs, Betty, her son, Dram, and grandson, Dash.

"Och, alright," Grace conceded, as they headed for the car. "Would you mind dropping the kids off with Eilidh?"

"I thought you were doing the drop off?" Paul asked with a light frown. "I said I'd help Angus with the deer afore we go for our final kilt fittings."

Over the last eighteen months, they had recently expanded into deer farming, and had a team of sixty red deer whom they farmed for venison.

"I've got to get to the bakery. I'm only open this morning, and I've to put the finishing touches to the wedding cake."

Paul relented with a good-natured sigh. "Aye, go on then. Come on kids, be quick. See you later."

He dropped a cool kiss on her cheek but Grace was already getting into the car.

"Love you all, see you later!"

With that, she waved, and headed off to the bakery.

Grace arrived at the Four Ducks bakery, named for her love of ducks, a short while later. It stood opposite the harbour, a prime spot for tourists as they arrived via ferry from the mainland, and was an impressive building, painted sage green, her favourite colour. As she parked the car, and walked along the promenade, her dark hair whipped around her face with the warm summer breeze, she listened to the cry of gulls, and smiled to herself as she glanced up at the wrought iron duck sign as she let herself in. She couldn't quite believe her luck, that she was now running her own bakery.

Grace's footsteps echoed on the dark grey wooden floor as she entered the bakery, and sighed with pleasure as she turned the sign to OPEN. In the centre of the room was a large counter, with the phone and till, a clear screened counter for the cakes, and along the walls, were the clippings of the Visit Scotland article and Grace's interview a few weeks later, as well as an award for Best New Business.

. . .

Last year, she had bitten the bullet and brought the old Mackay building at auction. Starting at Christmas, she and her husband Paul had renovated the old sweet shop, which reminded her of one in a Roald Dahl book, due to it being tall and imposing. Over the past twelve weeks, they had installed new ovens, shelving, flooring and had painted the walls a bright shade of emerald green, with gold ducks stencilled along the walls. So far, it had all gone smoothly: the installation had gone well, the decoration was just as she had wanted.

Heading into the back to the little emerald-green and gold tiled kitchenette, Grace went to the cupboard above the full green and chrome range, and collected the ingredients for the orange blossom honey cakes. These were one of her most popular batches since the article had come out, turned the oven to the right temperature, and then laid the ingredients out on the counter next to the oven where she placed a large pan. Honey cakes were her favourite thing to bake and were a staple for birthdays and at Christmas, reminding her of baking on a weekend with her mother.

Adding the butter to the pan with the orange blossom honey and dark brown sugar, she heated it up and melted it, stirring them together until the butter was melted. The scent of orange blossom wafted up from the pan and that made her smile.

Once it was melted, she turned off the heat and let the mixture cool whilst she got out and lined and greased a muffin tin. Once the mixture was cool enough, she added the eggs and mixed them in. Putting a large mixing bowl on the counter, she sieved in self-raising flour, and poured the egg, honey and sugar mixture into the bowl, mixing it until the mixture was runny. Pouring it into the cake tin, she was adding them to the oven when the phone on the counter out front burst into life.

"Good morning, Four Ducks Bakery, how may I help you? Yes, that's right, we make custom cakes. What did you have in mind? That sounds wonderful. Yes. I can sort that for you..." Grace asked in her best telephone voice. As she took the call, she admired the view of the harbour through the front windows, the stone walled harbour and the approaching ferries, and her face cracked into a smile as she watched the view now.

The sun was shining bright, and the waves were crashing gently against the harbour wall. As she glanced across at the harbour, and saw the ferry pull to a halt and watched as a group of tourists make their way up the ramp, Grace's face cracked into a smile. The small group of ten, who were all dressed in anoraks, hiking boots and bobble hats, and backpacks, stepped off the ferry and made their way towards the shop. One was holding a map, and was pointing in the bakery direction, and the group headed as one towards the shop.

. . .

"Alright, thank you. If you'll like to email us, we'll sort out all the details. Thank you," Grace said as she ended the call and turned as the shop bell peeled.

Just in time, she thought to herself with a smile, and smoothed her dress, keen to make a good impression. Welcoming customers still made her nervous, and the need to impress them made her feel jittery.

"Is this the award winning Four Ducks Bakery?" asked one of the group, and Grace nodded, unable to stop a broad smile crossing her face. Since the release of the Visit Scotland article and interview, and the welcome of warm weather, Mossbrae had had a surge in tourists visiting, and as a result, trade had expanded many businesses including Cairnmhor Honey, and Four Ducks Bakery. She had also received a surge in followers to the bakery's Instagram page and had been run off her feet with more and more orders. It had had a knock-on effort for an increase in people wanting honey, much to Angus and Eilidh's delight, which had brought much needed revenue, and allowing them to plan the wedding of their dreams.

"Aye, it is. How can I help you?"

"We heard about you in the Visit Scotland article, and we follow you on Instagram," one of the tourists, an elderly lady in a red bobble hat, exclaimed, waving a booklet.

"We heard this is the best bakery in the Inner Hebrides," added another lady. "I've heard your orange blossom honey cakes are the best?"

"Well just between us I cannae recommend them

enough!" Grace replied, her face breaking into a smile. It always give her a thrill of happiness when anyone complimented the bakery. "I've just got a batch in the oven. I'll go and get them for you."

She went into the back and got the cakes out of the oven, drizzling the orange blossom honey onto them as she put them onto the tray and carried them out, filling the bakery with the delicious, sweet scent of the cakes.

The tourist's faces lit up with delight as she brought them out and put them onto the counter.

"Please, help yourselves."

Each one of the group took one and she watched with satisfaction as their faces changed from delighted wonder to sheer joy. One or two tourists even closed their eyes and savoured them.

"Oh, my goodness!" a middle aged lady in a red bobble hat gasped. "They are delicious! Could we take some away with us?"

"Aye, of course. Take this batch. I'll put them in a Tupperware box for you."

"Thank you so much!" The lady cried. "Where did you get the honey? I'd love to buy some."

"The honey is locally sourced from Cairnmhor Honey, run by my brother and his fiancée."

"They run the business from their home, but their honey is available at the Cairnmhor Farm shop. It's about a ten minute drive from here."

"Aye, we've heard of them from the Visit Scotland article!" Another of the group cried excitedly. We all follow you on Instagram."

"Do you really? That's wonderful!"

"We love your posts!" Gushed another tourist, a teenager wearing a dark navy striped anorak. "They're so inspiring. I want to open my own bakery too."

"Thanks," Grace replied, feeling her cheeks flush with happiness.

"Can we get blackberry honey from the farm shop too?"

"Aye, you can."

"Can we look around the farm?"

"I'm afraid not, as it is a working farm."

"What's it like growing up on the farm?"

"It's very busy," Grace replied.

"Are there beekeeping courses we can go on?" Someone else asked. "I know a little bit about beekeeping."

"Oh, my brother's fiancée is the beekeeper. She is thinking of running classes in the future. I'll be sure to mention it to her."

"They're getting married soon, aren't they? How is the cake coming along?"

"Aye, they are. The cake is coming along nicely."

"Can we come to the wedding?" Someone joked. "We'd love to see the cake in person."

"I'll be sure to post it on Instagram once it's finished," Grace replied, trying not to laugh. "I've still got to add the finishing touches."

"Well, we're going to go and visit the farm shop. We'll be sure to buy a lot of honey. We love supporting small businesses."

"Thank you so much!"

"Thank you for the cakes!" The group called as they began to leave.

"No worries!" Grace called as she showed them out, watching them head towards their mini bus. Usually she charged customers for the cakes but today, she didn't mind a one off freebie. Not when they had assured her that they would buy some honey from the farm shop.

When they were gone, Grace let out a long sigh. She hadn't even intended to open up today, wanting to focus on the wedding preparation but she was glad she did. But she wasn't going to stay afloat very long if she didn't keep open for the customers. At the same time though, she felt more than a little exhausted. Rubbing her eyes with tiredness and stifling a yawn, she walked back into the kitchenette. Her time at the bakery had been none stop since the article, she had been run off her feet, fulfilling orders for specialised custom cakes, and spent every day in the bakery, meeting and greeting tourists. She loved it, but secretly she was looking forward to a much needed weekend off.

She went to the cupboard and got the wedding cake down. Even though it wasn't quite finished, she smiled to herself with satisfaction. The three tiered cake was vanilla sponge rather than traditional fruit, and was decorated with vanilla icing, and dark chocolate and vanilla buttercream. She breathed in the scent of vanilla and dark chocolate, which made her mouth water. As she looked at the cake, her mind went back to Eilidh's first wedding to her ex, Jack. Grace realised now, that it wasn't until she had finished that cake, a three tier fruit cake, with traditional white icing, and without anything fancy, that she realised that it had reflected their relationship and she thought it hinted at their incompatibility. Especially when had had left her for his ex-girlfriend, jilting Eilidh on the day of their wedding.

It wouldn't be like that for Eilidh and Angus though. Especially once she'd added the finishing touches...

She went to the other cupboard, and got out her her icing kit and four bags of rolled icing in green, white yellow and black, and set them out on the counter. Then, she began to work her magic. Rolling out the green icing, she rolled it across the top layer of the cake, making little sprigs and adding them sporadically to make it look like freshly mown grass. Turning to the white and black icing, she cut out tiny circles and rolled them into spheres, adding tiny rolled legs and smiled as the white and black became tiny sheep. Then, she rolled out the yellow and black, twisting it into a tiny beehive, and three tiny honeybees.

Then she turned and pulled out the short step ladder which she kept down the side of the counter, and placed the top tier on top of the other two. Then, she got tweezers, sugar silver balls, and delicate iced flowers which she set out on the counter. Collecting a sugar ball with the tweezers, she carefully picked one up and placed it on the top tier. Grace prided herself on having a delicate hand, as she placed the sugar balls and iced flowers along the side of the tier.

When she was finished a couple of hours later, she stepped back and admired the cake, and took out her phone she took a couple of photographs, planning to post them to Instagram later. It reflected both Angus and Eilidh's personalities perfectly. She couldn't wait to see their reactions. Feeling emotion well up now, she knew that she wanted more than anything for Angus and Eilidh to find true happiness, and for their wedding day to be the one everyone remembered. After all the struggle for them to get together, they deserved a happy ending, and she was determined to give them that through the means she could: a cake to remember, and which would truly make their big day.

The cake wouldn't just be one to remember, it would be the centre piece of the perfect wedding day. She would make sure of it.

Chapter Two

*A*t Honeybee Cottage, the air was filled with birdsong and the heady scent of buddleia and the gentle hum of honeybees as Eilidh opened the hive, ready for her weekly inspections. It was almost the height of the honey season, which was one of Eilidh's favourite times of year. Eilidh had been a beekeeper since her early teens, having had lessons like this one with her late grandmother and mentor, Marianne, in this very back garden. Upon her passing, Eilidh had inherited the cottage and now, to have bee keeping lessons here, felt like keeping the tradition alive. It made her almost tearful as she was hit with a stab of nostalgia, as she glanced around at the hives, the buddleia, and her Mhairi and Ollie, her niece and nephew, keen to begin their learning.

"Today, we are gonnae check the hives, and inspect the honey supers," Eilidh, dressed in her lavender bee suit and veil, asked the kids, who were stood nearby, dressed in identical bee suits.

"But before we do that, what do we need to do? It's very important. Does anyone remember?"

"Me!" Mhairi called, waving her hand. "We need to tell the bees!"

"That's right!" Eilidh replied. "What does 'telling the bees' mean?"

"Telling them big news," Ollie said knowledgeably.

"Like your and Uncle Gus's wedding!" Mhairi piped up.

"Why do we need to tell them?"

Mhairi glanced at Ollie and shrugged. Ollie glanced over at the hives and shook his head.

"I cannae remember..." Mhairi murmured, shuffling her feet.

"It is to stop the bees from leaving the hive," Eilidh explained, as Marianne had once explained to her. "It's a tradition famed in parts of Europe and Great Britain that bees were informed of an event, a marriage, a birth, and especially a death. You knock on the hive, and announce that their keeper has died, but that they must no' go for their new master will take care of them. For weddings, you place a piece of wedding cake near the hive for the bees, and you wrap a garland around the hive. So, shall we tell them about the wedding?"

Cautiously, the kids approached the hive. Ollie tentatively knocked on the hive and then Mhairi took a step forward, cupping her hands so that the bees could hear her.

"Aunty Eilidh and Uncle Gus are getting married!"

They stood back, beaming and Eilidh felt tears of happiness spring to her eyes.

"That was brilliant. Well done."

"I cannae wait to be a bridesmaid!" Mhairi piped up.

"You're gonnae be a lovely bridesmaid."

"Ma said you're going on honeymoon. What's a honeymoon?" Ollie asked.

"A holiday for the bees!" Mhairi piped up excitedly and Eilidh couldn't help but smile.

"A honeymoon is a holiday you go on after you get married," she explained.

"Are you taking the bees?" Ollie asked.

"No, we cannae take the bees with us," Eilidh smiled.

"Can we go?" Mhairi asked.

"I'm afraid not. It'll just be me and Uncle Angus."

"I thought you were already married?" Ollie frowned, looking confused. "Ma said it's about time. 'Cause you took so long to get together."

Eilidh shook her head. "Aye, well, we were friends for a long time and then we fell in love." She and Angus were childhood friends, having grown up together. They had remained friends, but it wasn't until she had moved back to Mossbrae and thanks to their friend's match-making, that she had realised their true feelings for each other.

"But no, we're getting married in a few week's time. In the Highlands. "

"Ma said you're getting married at Cousin Rory's. He lives in a castle!" Ollie exclaimed with excitement.

"Are you getting married in a castle? Like a princess?" Mhairi asked.

"Well, it's a mansion, so it's sort of a castle…"

Thanks to Angus's cousin, Rory, they were getting married at his grand Georgian estate in the Scottish Highlands.

"Is there gonnae be a frog?" Mhairi asked.

"A frog? No, there isnae a frog," Eilidh replied, suppressing a chuckle.

"I like frogs."

Ollie glanced at the hives and back at Eilidh. "Did you ask Uncle Angus on a date or did he ask you?"

"He asked me."

"I'm gonnae ask my friend Sally to the school disco."

"That's brave of you," Eilidh said proudly. "I bet she'll love to go with you."

"Is Sally your girlfriend?" Mhairi asked.

"No. She's my friend."

"I've got a boyfriend."

"You're five!" Ollie snorted.

"So? You're seven! Kerr and me are gonnae get married. Aunty Eilidh, can you be my bridesmaid?"

"I'd love that," Eilidh said.

"Is Aunty Robyn gonnae bring her baby to the wedding?"

"Aye, she will be. Well, the baby hasnae been born yet."

"Why?" Mhairi asked with a frown.

"Well, babies take a long time to grow."

"Aunty Eilidh, where do babies come from?" Mhairi asked aloud.

Eilidh looked flustered and was about to answer when Ollie came to her rescue.

"They come from flowers," Ollie replied. "Ma told me. Is that true, Aunty Eilidh?" Ollie asked.

"Ah, well…"

"Are you and Uncle Angus gonnae have a baby?" Mhairi asked.

"Aye, I hope so. One day…" Eilidh replied. "Now shall we start the inspection?"

Both kids nodded enthusiastically, and she smiled at them with pride at their enthusiasm. The kids were showing more of an interest in beekeeping with each lesson, and were proving themselves keen learners with a natural love of bees and nature.

"First we use the smoker to calm the bees as we open the hive," Eilidh explained as she moved the smoker across the hive, and opened the lid. "First, we remove the cover board, and because it's on the top we inspect the honey super first."

"And collect any honey!" Mhairi added excitedly.

"Aye, that's right," Eilidh nodded. "So what do we need to do?"

"We need to use the bee brush," Mhairi replied. "To move the bees away."

"Aye, that's right!"

Eilidh continued moving the bees gently with a sweep of her brush.

Next, she removed the clearer board. The clearer

board kept the bees inside the brood box so that it was safe to remove the honey supers. Then, Eilidh lifted out a frame from the honey super, which was the box where all the bees made the honey.

"So this is a frame," Eilidh explained. "What do the bees use the frames for?"

"To make honey, and to lay eggs on the ones in the brood box," Ollie said.

"That's right!" Eilidh replied. "So what can you see?"

"There's honey there!" Ollie exclaimed.

"That's wonderful!" Eilidh replied. "What do we need to do next?"

"We need to swap the frames out for fresh ones," Ollie said.

"Ollie! I was gonnae say that!" Mhairi cut in.

"Aye, you can both tell me the answers," Eilidh replied. "Ollie, can you hand me the frames, and Mhairi, can you pass the bag for the frames?"

Ollie stepped forward and handed Eilidh the fresh frames, and Mhairi handed over the bag to put the old frames in.

"That's grand, thank you. Right, next we check the brood box," Eilidh instructed. "We do weekly inspections during the honey season. In May and June, the bees are more likely to swarm. We may need to split the hive to make a new colony."

They continued the check on the hive before moving to the honey supers, which Eilidh had removed in order to get to the brood box at the bottom.

Opening the hive, Eilidh lifted another frame. "Any swarming?"

The kids paused. "There's lots of bees!" Mhairi said.

"We do we need to look out for?" Eilidh asked.

"The June Gap!"

The June Gap was a lull in the honey season when there was a risk of losses, and there was less for bees to forage to make honey, leading to them eating the honey they had stored.

"So how do we deal with that?"

"Check the weather! To make sure the bees don't swarm."

Eilidh nodded. "How do we stop them swarming?"

"We create an artificial swarm," Ollie said knowledgeably.

"Aye? How do we do that?"

"We use the nuc."

A nuc was the shortened version of a nucleus colony, a small sized hive in which you kept a small colony of bees. Nucs were used when splitting a hive, and when introducing a new colony to a new hive.

Eilidh pulled the nuc out and opened it up. "So to create an artificial swarm, we need to catch the Queen."

"She's marked in blue!" Mhairi piped up and Eilidh nodded.

"Aye, that's right. So we have our Queen capture. We catch the Queen, and then, we open up the hive."

Eilidh proceeded to walk the kids through the process of creating an artificial swarm. Once the Queen was removed and placed in a nuc to create a new colony, Eilidh went through the hive and removed all the Queen egg cells, the enlarged ones, which would stop creating a cast swarm, where the bees left the hive with a virgin Queen, leaving the hive abandoned.

In order to encourage the bees to create a new Queen, the hive would be left for a week, then any more Queen cells would be removed except one, and then the hive again would be left again for four weeks. This would ensure enough time would have passed to ensure the new Queen had have mated and started laying eggs to strengthen the hive and get the numbers back up, without interfering with any honey production at the same time.

Next, Eilidh removed two frames from the hive and placed them in the nuc. One frame of stores and pollen to feed the new hive (this one would not produce honey until the following year) and one of sealed eggs, (not unsealed because the bees needed a one day old egg to produce a new queen.) Then, she shook two frames worth of bees into the nuc (most of which would be nurse bees who would stay in the nut and tend to the sealed brood,) and the flying bees would fly back to the hive and continue as normal.

Soon, Eilidh finished her checks and the bee keeping lesson came to an end.

"Let's wrap it up now, your Ma will be here soon

and we need to get your outfits sorted for the wedding. Let's wash your hands. Next time, we'll learn how to extract the honey and put it into jars. Then we'll learn how to make honey cakes using the honey we've extracted."

The kids cheered and Eilidh closed the hives, and they headed inside to clean up.

"You're great at beekeeping, Aunty Eilidh..." Mhairi piped up. "When I grow up, I want to be a beekeeper, just like you!"

"Thank you, that's a lovely thing to say. I'd like that too. You're going to make a grand beekeeper. Next time, "

She turned her attention one last time to the hives in the garden now, hit by a sudden wave of nostalgia. She could almost see her late grandmother, Marianne, in her bee suit, and hear her voice as she tended to the hives as she used to do when she was a child, as she told her the same thing about wanting to be a beekeeper all those years ago...

Chapter Three

he Past.

Beltane.

The hum of bees filled the air as Marianne Andersen, dressed in her bee suit, completed the checks on her hives that morning. It had been a busy morning and she was looking forward to finishing early. Today was Beltane, the festival for the celebration of spring, and also her godmothers' (Enid, Nelly and Maudie, aka The Trinity on account they were triplets) birthday party, where they were holding the Beltane celebrations.

"I cannae believe you've never been to a Beltane party before," Marianne said to Annabelle as they drove down the country roads towards The Trinity's home, The Stables.

"Am I overdressed?" Annabelle asked, glancing down at her pink gingham sundress and pink cardigan. "Should I have worn jeans?"

"No, you look braw," said Marianne brightly. She was wearing a lime green mini dress and sandals, her long light brown hair dancing around her shoulders in Farah Fawcett waves.

"What are they like?" Annabelle asked as they approached the farm and Marianne parked up. "Enid, Maudie and Nelly?"

"Och, they're braw. You'll love them. Maudie is the eccentric sister, she had candy floss pink hair, Enid is the sensible one, and Nelly is the fun loving one. They'r wonderful. They love a good gossip and match making."

"Two of my favourite things!" Annabelle giggled.

"Marianne!"

Marianne looked up to see a tall, blonde woman walking towards her as the arrived at The Stables.

"Maudie!" Marianne cried, throwing her arms wide and enveloping her in a bear hug. "How great to see you. How have you been?"

"Grand. We've been grand. I hear you're losing your accent a bit! You need to come home more often."

"Aye. I will try. It's so much fun being away at college."

Both Marianne and Annabelle were away at colleague on the mainland.

Maudie, whose candy floss pink hair was loose at the shoulders gave a chuckle. She was in her early forties- forty two today to be precise. She and her two other sisters were celebrating their birthday with the arrival of Beltane. As always they were throwing a party in the lower fields, where Marianne and Annabelle could already see a massive bonfire roaring.

"There's a bonfire…" Annabelle whispered and Marianne laughed.

"There's always a bonfire. It's a farming tradition for welcoming spring," said Enid now, her own blonde hair cut into a neat bob just below her jawline as she walked past them towards the kitchen. She was the middle triplet, and the stoic, serious one who wore thick, heavy spectacles on the end of her nose.

"Where's Nelly?"

"Pouring the drinks, I dinnae doubt," said Maudie cheerfully. "Enid, you remember Marianne's friend, Annabelle?"

"Aye, hello," Enid said, sounding distracted. "Nice to meet you both."

"Come and mingle," said Maudie. "Can I offer you a drink?"

"Have you got any of that lovely punch?" Marianne asked and Maudie nodded enthusiastically.

"Aye, we always make the dandelion punch. It's made from actual dandelions."

"Really?" Annabelle asked as they walked through the house, admiring the decor and the long trellis table laid out with a delicious array of food and drink.

"It's delicious," Marianne replied. "I'll get you a glass..."

She headed to the table and picked up two glasses, ladeling in two labels of punch.

"Here you go."

"Thanks," Annabelle said tentatively, and took a cautious sip. It was sweet, with a tangy aftertaste and Annabelle found that she liked it.

"It's braw, aye?" Marianne replied and Annabelle nodded.

"It is."

"I told you it would be" Marianne said, and beckoned for her to follow her outside. "Let's go and see the bonfire."

Annabelle followed her outside to where a crowd had gathered, admiring the bonfire.

"It's braw, aye?" Marianne said. "I love to come back for The Trinity's birthday and enjoy the Beltane celebrations."

"Why is there so much fire?"

"It symbolises new life," Marianne explained. "To

welcome the coming of Spring. hence the bonfires. It is traditional to move cattle and sheep during these times, and I often move the beehives too. It's supposed to bring good luck."

"Thats a brilliant tradition," Annabelle replied.

"It's also," Marianne added conspiratorially with a wink. "A great place to find a boyfriend."

"Och! Behave!" Annabelle chuckled. "You know I'm not looking for anyone. I'm happy being single."

"Aye? Is that so?" Marianne teased. "Well that's a shame. I've heard there's gonnae be a few rather handsome lads here tonight."

"Who? Friends of yours?" Annabelle asked.

"Aye. Well, they live in the neighbouring farms. One of them is Joe Kincaid."

"He lives across at Cairnmhor farm?" Annabelle said, recalling the name now. "His family has run the hill farm for the last four generations. He's doing well for himself."

"Dinnae fancy being a farmer's wife?"

Annabelle gave a nonchalant shrug. "I've never thought about it."

This of course, was a lie. She had often wondered what it would be like to stay in Mossbrae, on one of the many farms dotted around the village. But she wasn't sure about the winters, and the hardship of running a farm.

Her mind went to Joe Kincaid now. He was around her age, maybe a few years older, dark, handsome, rugged, a bit of a Jack the Lad some said, but she'd liked him the few times they had crossed paths in The Dog and Duck, but she hadn't spoken to him, not properly at least.

"What time are they getting here?" Annabelle asked casually, checking her watch. It was almost six pm and her stomach was already rumbling.

"Not until later, probably," Marianne said. "Being farmers they work all hours. There's a lot of new lambs to look after at the moment."

"I love lambs," Annabelle said. She wasn't just saying that. There was something wonderful about the bleating of lambs calling to their mothers on a warm spring day.

"Come on then," Marianne said, nudging her and Annabelle realised she was staring at the door, waiting for him to arrive.

"Let's get some food whilst we wait."

"Aye. Let's," said Annabelle, tuning to follow her.

There was a delicious selection of food laid out, with a spiced roast leg of lamb and a tureen of vegetable broth made with carrots, turnips and potatoes.

"This looks delicious!" Annabelle exclaimed as Nelly dished out the lamb broth and vegetables.

"Thank you," said Annabelle as she took a seat and tucked in. It was well seasoned and delicious, and Annabelle was just drinking the broth at the bottom of the bowl when she looked up and spotted him.

"Oops!" She gasped, dropping broth down her dress, and dabbed futilely at it with a napkin.

"Joe!" Marianne called excitedly, giving Annabelle a knowing look. "You made it."

"Aye. I wouldnae miss a good Beltane party," Joe replied, as he shrugged off his black leather jacket. He was more rugged than Annabelle remembered, his eyes and hair dark as night, and she felt her stomach flutter at the sight of him.

"Annabelle's here," said Marianne, and Joe turned his attention to her now, smiling at her warmly as he extended his hand.

"Hello again, Annabelle. How are you? Happy Beltane."

"Hello, Joe." Said Annabelle, hoping he didn't notice the stain on the front of her dress. "Nice to meet you again. Happy Beltane."

She regarded him a little awkwardly, aware he was drinking her in, his dark gaze fixed on hers, and she tried not to blush.

"I see you've finished eating," Joe said. "Fancy a dance?"

"I'd like that, thank you," said Annabelle, nodding. "That'd be lovely."

Taking her hand and leaving the bowl in the centre of the table, Joe lead her outside to where a makeshift dance floor had been made from hay bales at one corner of the field.

Joe lead her to the centre, surrounded by several other guests.

"How have you been?" Joe asked as they began to dance. "I havenae seen you around for a while."

"Aye, I've been away at college," Annabelle replied as he took her hand, and put his other around her waist, and she found herself blushing at the warm roughness of his hand.

"How about you? I hear you've got some lambs at Cairnmhor right now."

"Aye. We've a few wee ones at the moment," said Joe. "You'll have to come over and see them afore you head back to college. What do you think?"

"Aye, I'd like that," Annabelle replied with a nod, realising she was looking forward to it, and wondering whether it was because she was going to get to spend time with him.

"We have a fun little tradition," Joe went on. "Whoever lambs the first crop of lambs gets to name them. If you want to have a try at lambing one, I'll let you name it."

"Me? Have a go at lambing?" Annabelle laughed.

"I could recruit you in the Kincaid School of Lambing if you like," Joe replied with an easy grin, and Annabelle burst out laughing.

"The Kincaid School of Lambing? Is that official?"

"Aye. It is now. You can be my first pupil."

Annabelle looked up at him, her gaze meeting his. Was he flirting with her? She hoped so.

"I'd like that," she replied, smiling back at him.

"We can start tomorrow if you like…"

· · ·

"What do you think?" Maudie, standing in the doorway, glancing at Enid and Nelly conspiratorially. "That's another match if ever I saw one…"

"Aye, I'll second that," said Marianne with a grin.

"What about you, Marianne?" Maudie asked, turning to her.

"Och, I've no-one in mind," Marianne said, shaking her head.

"You've not met the right one yet," said Enid solemnly. "A stranger will cross your path and you will meet the one for you before long…"

"Aye?" Marianne asked, raising an eyebrow. She wasn't exactly sceptical of The Trinity's power of predicting the future, but she was a little unnerved by their accuracy.

"One match at a time, I think," Nelly interjected. "Though, saying that, I'd highly recommend matchmaking."

"After all, you and Albert were the subject of match-making," Maudie added proudly.

"Aye," said Nelly, nodding over to her husband, Albert. He was a short, square man, who was the opposite of Nelly, but they made a wonderful team. Albert was from farming stock like her, and was a cattle farmer. He was hoping to set up a farm himself in Ireland, but for now, he was content to stay at the Stables, and help maintain their family home.

"There's plenty of time to find a match for you," Enid said gently, and went back into the dining room to get some food.

. . .

"Are you seeing anyone?" Joe asked as he spun Annabelle around the dance floor.

"No. Are you?"

"No. I havnae found time to meet anyone," said Joe, still looking at her. "I'm run off my feet with helping out on the farm. Plus, I dinnae know if you knew, but in Mossbrae, there are fewer lasses than lads. I wouldnae be able to find a girlfriend that easily..." he kept his gaze on her.

"So, there's no handsome city boys you have your eye on?"

"No. I'm happily single."

Joe took her hands.

"Spin with me," he said, as they danced. "Count the beats..."

They spun in a circle, and Annabelle couldn't help but burst out laughing. "This is a lot of fun."

"Aye. We should do this again. When are you free?"

"I come back at the end of Summer term."

"That's only a few weeks away," Joe said evenly. "I can wait that long to secure a date with you, I suppose. And by summer, all the lambing will be over and done with."

"Do you get a lot of free time in summer?" Annabelle asked.

"Not that much, but I'll have enough time to take you out for a date or two. A drink and dinner down The

Dog and Duck some time," Joe replied, smiling at her. "What do you think?"

"Are you asking me out?"

"Aye, go on then."

Annabelle glanced up and meeting his gaze, felt her face flame at the way he was looking at her in that intense, alluring way.

"I like you, Annabelle Gordon," Joe announced.

"I like you," Annabelle admitted, and before she could stop herself, she stepped forwards and kissed him.

"She doesnae hang about!" Maudie chuckled from her vantage point by the patio.

"Och, you can say that again," Nelly laughed, fanning herself. "How many glasses of that punch has she had?"

"Just enough," Marianne grinned. "She's had a crush on Joe Kincaid for the last couple of months."

"Aye? And he likes her from what we can see…"

Maudie and Nelly grinned. "Well, it looks like we're right with another one…"

The following day Annabelle made her way to Cairnmhor Farm.

"Morning, lass!" Angus Snr, Joe's father greeted her warmly. "Looking for Joe?"

"Aye. He said he was gonnae show me the lambs."

"He's in the lambing barn at the moment," Angus Senior replied. He was tall and broad like Joe himself was, and but where Joe had dark eyes, Angus Sr's were blue, and he had a weathered look about him which she could see would be appealing.

"Thank you," Annabelle called, and headed towards the lambing barn.

Inside it was much louder than she had expected, the sounds of ewes baaing to their lambs filled the small barn. The scent of lanolin and straw was welcoming, and she glanced around, looking for Joe.

"Annabelle?"

She heard his voice from over the far side, and she turned, waving.

"Over here, this ewe's just started. Fancy a go?"

Annabelle nodded, making her way across the straw towards him, eyeing the sheep warily. She hadn't been so close to sheep before and they looked quite intimidating with the way they stared and observed you.

"They willnae hurt you, lass," Joe assured her as she reached him, and Annabelle looked down at his overalls now, glad she was wearing jeans and a lemon yellow seater, as it was a fresh morning, her corn blonde hair was fastened into a neat plait, a change from the Farah Fawcett hairstyle she had worn last night.

"Right," Joe began, indicating for her to roll up her sleeves. "Ready for your first lesson?"

"Aye, I am," said Annabelle with a nod.

"This is how you check for the lamb," Joe explained, as he checked. "What you're looking for is the two front legs and the muzzle."

"Right," Annabelle said tentatively, and copied him.

"Oh! That is a strange sensation. I'm not hurting the ewe, am I?"

Joe shook his head. "No. She's too busy trying to get the lamb out."

"Is there just one lamb?"

"Aye. She's a single. She's a glimmer, meaning she's a two year old sheep, so this is her first lamb..."

He checked the ewe was calm, and then carried on. "Can you feel the feet and muzzle?"

Annabelle nodded.

"Now, the lamb is in the right position. The lamb needs to be born as though it is diving."

"Aye..."

"Right, so you grab the feet and gently tug the lamb out on the next contraction... I'll count you in. Ready? Three, two, one, now gently tug..."

"The feet are slippy."

"You have to hold quite hard," Joe said, unfazed. "Now, pull."

Annabelle pulled the lamb, and soon enough, the lamb was born.

"Ah! I did it!" Annabelle cried, and laughed a little unsteadily. "I lambed a lamb!"

"Well done," Joe said softly. "You've passed with flying colours! What are you gonnae call her?"

"I'm gonnae call her Lavender."

"A grand name," Joe said, and as his gaze met hers, he leant in and kissed her.

"How would you fancy being a farmer's wife?" Joe asked.

"Are you serious?" Annabelle gasped.

"Aye. I think I am," Joe replied. "I know we've barely had a date as such, but I'm dinnae want to fool around with the wrong girl. I'm looking to marry."

"I'm looking for something serious too," Annabelle replied honestly. "So, yes. I'll marry you…"

Chapter Four

resent Day.

"Aunty Eilidh!"

Eilidh jolted from her memories, turning to hear the doorbell.

"How did the beekeeping lessons go?" Grace asked as she opened the door.

"We had a wonderful time," Eilidh replied. "All ready for the bridesmaid fitting. Mhairi is very excited."

"What time is Jeannie arriving?"

"Any moment, I should think. She's catching the ferry and a taxi," Eilidh replied. "I'll put a brew on whilst we're waiting. I hope she finds the journey well. She said other than the fittings, she doesnae take the ferry often."

"Aye, that's a grand idea. The sea wasnae choppy

this morning, so it should be a smooth crossing," Grace said, following her.

"Can we make honey cakes after?" Mhairi asked.

"Not today, hen," she replied, placing a hand on her shoulder. "We've a lot to do afterwards. Da has to go for a kilt fitting with Uncle Gus, and Grandad."

"Can we look after the sheep whilst they're gone?" Ollie asked.

"You can keep an eye on the ducks," Grace said firmly.

Eilidh went into the kitchen.

"Can you help me move this dining table? Jeannie likes the space when she's doing a fitting."

"Aye," Grace agreed, and together, they moved the dining table and chairs to one side, creating enough room for Jeannie to get to work.

Of all the rooms at Honeybee Cottage, the kitchen had the best natural light, and Jeannie liked to make the most of the of it, especially on a bright, sunny day like today.

"There," she announced once they had moved the dining chairs to one side, and she smiled to herself. "I cannae believe this is gonnae be the final dress fitting!"

"Aye, the times goes quick," Grace smiled back. "Only a week to go."

"There seems so much to do yet, the kilts, the dresses, there's the Dooking…"

An ancient Highland pre-wedding tradition where

the bride and groom were covered with a variety of things.

"Och, dinnae fret about that bit," Grace's face broke into a grin. "That's all sorted..."

"Aye?" Eilidh asked with a raised eyebrow."

The doorbell rang, and Eilidh hurried down the hallway to answer it.

"Morning!These are all for you. Not long til the big day, aye?"

It wasn't Jeannie, it was the postman, who was holding a several small boxes, and an armful of cards and letters.

"Thank you! Aye, just a week to go," she replied brightly, and gingerly took them from him, not wanting to drop anything, calling thanks and goodbye as she closed the door with her foot.

"Wow! Are they all for you and Uncle Gus?" Mhairi cried in delight, as Eilidh carried them to the kitchen table to check them.

"Aye, it seems so," she replied as she spread them out across the table, separating wedding post from bills. "Och, there's a telegram... Ah, it's from Jim. How lovely!"

She opened it now, and read it aloud.

"Dear Eilidh and Angus. Wishing you all the best for your wedding day. Have a wonderful time. I knew you two were made for each other when I met you at the sales and I'm so glad you're finally tying the knot. All the best, from Jim and family. Och, that's wonderful! Thank you, Jim."

She felt tears of happiness spring to her eyes as she put the rest of the wedding cards to one side to one on the big day, and turned to the presents, looking at the post mark.

"Ah, it's here!" Eilidh cried in delight. "Mhairi, Ollie, come here!"

Ollie and Mhairi rushed into the kitchen from the garden now, and watched in wonder as she lifted the headdress for Mhairi and mini button hole for Ollie from the box.

"What do you think?" she asked, turning to them now with a smile.

"They're beautiful!" Mhairi crowed in delight. "Thank you, Aunty Eilidh!"

Eilidh lifted them out now, admiring her own stroke of luck at finding the head dress on Etsy. The headdress was cream, matching Mhairi's dress, embroidered by hand with thistles, and pressed flowers, and even a honeybee, which, she thought now, looked almost real. Even better, it matched her own veil.

"Och, that's braw, hen," Grace gasped. She turned to the buttonhole now, a thistle with a honeybee, and sighed with pure happiness. "They're gonnae look wonderful."

"Aye, I know," Eilidh replied with pride. "Just wait until we get them in their outfits! I cannae wait."

"Makes it all a little more real."

"It does."

They smiled at each other now as there was the beep of a car horn outside.

"Stay here, I'll get the door, you put the kettle on," Grace said gently, and left the kitchen.

As she made the tea, Eilidh heard the high pitched Highland tone of Jeannie's voice, as Grace greeted her and she couldn't help but smile.

"Here's the bride!" Jeannie called as she entered the kitchen. She was ninety-two, thin and wiry, reminding Eilidh of a Border Terrier.

"How was the journey?" She asked as she pulled her into a tight hug.

"Verra pleasant," Jeannie beamed, as she settled herself into one of the dining chairs.

"Brew?" Eilidh asked, turning to her. "Three sugars, wasn't it?"

"Ah, you remembered! Aye, three please," Jeannie replied. "A brew afore we start will put us in the right mood."

She made the tea, and handed it to Jeannie, who took a delighted sip.

"Ah, perfect!"

Jeannie sipped her tea, and Eilidh and Grace joined her.

"Have we any honey cakes?"

"No, afraid no, we've run out of honey," Grace replied, shaking her head.

"You should have said!" Eilidh cut in. "I've got plenty in the shed."

"I'd love one of those hampers I've heard about," Jeannie replied. "I read the Visit Scotland article. Verra well done, Grace."

"Thank you," Grace beamed, feeling proud of herself.

"Ma!" Mhairi and Ollie came rushing in from the garden. "Can we have our bridesmaid fitting yet?"

"We are just having a brew," Jeannie said in her prim voice, and smiled sweetly at her. "Then, we can work. Would you like a piece of tablet? I've brought some with me."

She opened her bag and removed a pink tissue paper wrapped parcel and removed the hard fudge, snapping off a piece and handing one of Mhairi and then to Ollie.

"Ooh! Thank you. I love tablet!" Mhairi said, taking a tentative nibble. It was sweet, crunchy, and delicious. Tablet was made of a boiled mix of sugar, milk, butter and condensed milk.

"Ma, can we make tablet in the shop?"

"Aye, that's an idea," Grace replied with a nod. "We could make different flavours."

"How about honey flavours," Eilidh added. "How about orange blossom honey flavour, or blackberry?"

"Och, that sounds braw!" Jeannie exclaimed. "How about that as an idea for wedding favours?"

She and Eilidh exchanged a delighted look.

"Jeannie, you're a genius!" Grace cried in delight. "What a wonderful idea!"

Her mind whirred now, thinking of all the flavours she could make, and wondering if she would have time.

"Right," Jeannie announced after the tablet was eaten, and the tea was drunk, pushing the chair back. "Time for the fitting."

They moved the chairs out of the way, and Jeannie gestured to Mhairi to come and sit on a dining chair.

"We'll do your dress first," she said as Mhairi sat obediently, and Grace watched with pride. The dress was cream, full length with lace capped sleeves, and detailing along the hem.

"Put your shoes on, hen," Jeannie instructed, and Mhairi did so, and did a twirl.

"What do you think?" she asked.

"You look wonderful!" Eilidh replied. "You're gonnae be the best bridesmaid ever!"

"Ollie, you're turn next, go and put your suit on," Grace prompted Ollie and he ran off to get changed.

"This is about the right length," Jeannie murmured, checking the dress length now, and nodded in approval. "There isnae much to do. Right, Mhairi, let's see with the headdress."

She put the headdress on, and did another twirl.

"Perfect!"

"I'm ready!" Ollie called, as he hurried back into the room, dressed in his smart suit. Grace added the button hole, and smiled at him proudly.

"Och, you look wonderful, son."

Ollie smiled proudly, as he stood in front of Jeannie now as she checked his jacket was the right length.

"Nothing to do here either. You two are all sorted."

"Right, shall I take these two home, Eilidh whilst you get your dress sorted, or do you want us to stay?" Grace asked.

"Stay," Eilidh replied with a wave of her hand. "I'm gonnae go and get the dress and veil…"

With that she left the kitchen and headed upstairs to her bedroom, and opened the wardrobe, admiring her wedding dress now.

The sight of it reminded her with sudden pain of her first wedding day, and her wedding dress. She couldn't help but cast her mind back to that Christmas Eve in an Edinburgh hotel three years ago, which had ended in her being jilted by Jack in favour of his ex-girlfriend, Sophie. Her dress had been the complete opposite, long sleeves, full skirted, and in hindsight, she realised, as she reached for her wedding dress now, entirely the wrong dress for her.

This dress was much more her… After all, she thought, glancing across at the photo of Marianne and Lars on their wedding day, and felt tears spring to her eyes, it had been Marianne's wedding dress. It was absolutely beautiful, with capped sleeves, and was full length, with embroidery along on the hem, similar to Mhairi's.

. . .

Eilidh lifted the dress off the hanger now, and changed into it, gently smoothing it. It looked wonderful, and she felt tears spring to her eyes as she was hit with a sudden wave of grief, especially when she went to the chest of drawers and took out the veil.

"This," Marianne's voice echoed in her head now as she recalled their conversation, all those years ago. "Was my wedding veil. I'd like you to have it when you decide to get married. If you want to, of course."

"It's beautiful!" Eilidh had exclaimed, as Marianne passed her the veil, lace, and embroidered with honey-bees and thistles. It had been hand-made by Marianne herself, and Eilidh knew she would treasure it forever.

"Thank you, Gran."

Eilidh found herself saying the words aloud as she held the veil between her fingers now, stroking the honeybees and thistles. She opened it now. and wiped the tears from her cheeks as she removed the veil, as she was hit by a fresh wave of grief. It felt as soft as it had done all those years ago, and she was certain she could smell the light scent of hyacinths…Years on, and it still felt as raw as yesterday…

Heading back downstairs, Eilidh carried the veil and her wedding shoes: low heeled gold court shoes and made her way back to the kitchen.

"Och, hen, you look a picture!" Grace exclaimed, and Eilidh felt her heart crunch at the sight of tears in her friend's eyes. "Angus is gonnae faint when he sees you."

"Let's hope after the vows!" Jeannie laughed as she turned to Eilidh now, helping her on with the veil.

"Is that Marianne's?" Grace asked as Eilidh nodded, and her eyes sparkled with tears. "It looks wonderful."

"You look just like her," Jeannie sighed and at that, Eilidh was hit by a wave of grief. Grace handed her a tissue to dab away the tears coursing down her cheeks, and Eilidh gave a loud sniff.

"Did you know Gran?" she asked Jeannie now.

"Aye of course, we Highland folk all know each other in one way or another. Marianne and I knew each other from school but grew apart when I moved out to the Outer Hebrides and my little bridal shop opened. But I was her seamstress for her wedding day, and I went to her wedding. It was a braw day… She was wonderful, was Marianne. When Maudie said you were getting married, I knew I had to come out of retirement to do Marianne's granddaughter's dress."

"Thank you," Eilidh replied, smiling through her tears, as Jeannie straightened her veil.

Eilidh glanced down at the dress, and felt emotion thicken her throat, and she couldn't wait to see the look on Angus's face.

"I wonder how the men are getting on with the kilt fitting?" she asked aloud, thinking of Angus in a kilt, and her heart skipped a beat, suddenly longing for their wedding day.

~

Harris' kilt shop had been open since Joe had hired a kilt for his own wedding fifty years ago. The shop was small, neatly arranged with rows of tartan kilts and waist coats, both traditional and modern, lining the walls, and a great selection, and had a welcoming presence, and decorated in suave shades of grey.

Despite it being in a prominent place on the high street, was a modest establishment, relying nowadays on the older generations of the village, who used it to hire kilts for Burn's Night, and Hogmanay.

As they entered the shop, Angus was taken back to their first kilt fitting three months earlier…

"Morning! Are you here for a fitting?" Ned Harris, great-grandson of the original owners, who now ran the shop, had called brightly as Angus, Joe and Paul walked in.

"Aye, we want to hire some kilts for an upcoming wedding," Joe replied proudly, clapping Angus on the shoulder.

"Ah, that's wonderful. What did you have in mind? Traditional or something a little more modern?"

"Traditional," Angus had affirmed. "We were gonnae go with family tartan, but we all want the groomsmen to all match."

"Ah, of course," said Ned, who was in his late twenties, and bespectacled, with carefully styled blond hair, turning an expert eye to the traditional tartans over by the changing rooms now. Choosing a tartan was a serious business, especially for a wedding, and he knew it had to be perfect. He had glanced over at Angus now, taking in the dark hair and eyes, rugged good looks, and outdoorsy profile.

"I think I have the perfect one for you!"

He had grabbed a dark green and navy blue kilt from the rack, a classic Gordon tartan, and presented it with a flourish.

Angus had regarded it now, feeling emotion rise in his own throat at the name as he exchanged a glance with knowing glance with Joe. His late mother Annabelle's maiden name had been Gordon.

"It looks braw, Son," said Joe, his face, lined with age, and slightly weather beaten, cracking into a smile as Angus emerged from into the changing room now, bringing him back to the present.

It looked great, the kilt falling to knee length, the colours suiting his dark hair and eyes. He had originally planned to wear the family Kincaid Tartan, which was similar colours, in honour of his father's side of the family, but somehow, honouring his mother's family name on his wedding day seemed more fitting, remembering her in her absence.

"We'd better try our's too," Joe asked, and Paul nodded. Ned had produced two more kilts and they tried them on, smiling at each other as they came out of the fitting room and cheered. Next was shirts, and waist-coats, a dark hunter's green to go with the kilt, and a classic white shirt underneath. On top were the jackets, dark navy, and when Angus caught sight of Joe's face, he saw tears welling in his pale blue eyes.

"Och, Da, are you alright?" Angus asked in concern, catching Joe's eyes as they stepped out of the changing room in all their finery.

Joe nodded. "All this reminds me of my own wedding all those years ago…"

He cast his mind back to that wintery day so close to Christmas, at St. Anthony's church. "Such a shame your Ma isnae here to celebrate it with us."

"I know," Angus said sadly, putting an arm around his shoulders. He tried not to take in how frail he looked. Joe hadn't been in the best health recently, but for a moment, he looked like he had done in his younger days as his eyes sparkled with youth as he smiled. "But she's here with us, in spirit."

"Aye, she is…"

Joe saw the memory of her in his mind, the corn-blonde hair, pale blue eyes and looking like a vision as she had entered the church, making her way down the aisle towards him. She had been fashionably late, and he had stood there in the draughty church, sweating despite the winter chill, and then, he had caught sight of her, and all the nerves had disappeared, replaced by pure love and happiness. "It was one of the best days of my life…" Joe said, wistfully, for a moment, lost in nostalgia and sat back to tell the others of his own wedding day and how romantic it had been… I'm so glad you've found The One for you too…"

Joe's gaze fixed on Angus's. "Eilidh is a wonderful girl. Your Ma and I couldnae be more proud."

"I'm so glad," Angus said, looking at his father now.

Chapter Five

 Week Later.

Eilidh sat in a deck chair in the back garden at Honeybee Cottage, enjoying the warmth of the sun on her skin so early in the morning. She loved summer mornings like this, with a cloudless, cerulean sky, and the scent of buddliea in the air, the hum of the honeybees. This morning, she was having a few moments peace before she started her work with the bees. As she breathed in the scent of roses, she was taken back to that day two years ago, when she had finally confessed her feelings for Angus, and he had for her.

Slowly, she took a sip of tea, feeling a flutter of excitement in the pit of her stomach at the realisation there was only two weeks until the wedding. She could hardly believe it… and she could hardly wait.

"Morning!"

She gave a yelp of surprise, spilling her tea as Robyn suddenly appeared next to her.

"Are you ready?" Robyn asked, her face pink with excitement.

"Ready?" Eilidh asked in confusion, glad she hadn't spilt tea on her clothes, and knowing the sun would dry it up by lunchtime.

"Dinnae tell me you've forgotten!" Robyn cried. "Hurry up! We've got a weekend planned, remember?"

"Och! Aye, of course!" Eilidh exclaimed, and hurried inside, grabbing her keys.

"She forgot. She was sitting in the garden, sunbathing," Robyn laughed, as Eilidh and she went out to the front, where Grace, Maudie, Enid, Nelly were squashed in the back of Robyn's car, waiting for them, and they let out a cheer when Eilidh and Robyn finally appeared.

Robyn climbed in the driver's seat, and Eilidh into the passenger seat, as she started the engine.

Grace rolled her eyes good naturally.

"I've been packed for weeks!" Nelly exclaimed with childish excitement. "I dinnae think I slept last night, I was so excited. A spa weekend away!"

They were heading to The Harbourside Hotel and Spa, on the mainland, a short ferry ride away, and before long, they were all aboard the car ferry, breathing in the salty sea air, and admiring the view as they made it across to the mainland. When she had found it online, Grace knew it would be the perfect place for a hen do

"We'd better get a move on or we'll miss the ferry," Grace replied.

Stepping into the soft carpeted lobby, with the smart reception desk and stairs leading up to the rooms and Eilidh felt a thrill that she was actually going to stay here. The views over the loch were amazing, and she was certain she had seen an osprey hunting fish as they drove along the country lane to the hotel.

"We've booked a suite, and we're also booked into the spa," Grace informed the receptionist, and she gave them instructions and towels.

"So what have you got planned for me?" Eilidh asked tentatively, as they walked through the double doors and up to their suite where they would all be staying for the weekend.

"First, we have a surprise for you!"

Grace exchanged a look with Robyn as they carried their bags upstairs.

Eilidh pressed her key card on the lock, and opened the door, giving a gasp of delight.

"Ma?"

Connie Andersen turned as Eilidh rushed into the room and embraced her.

"I thought you couldn't make it until the wedding?" she exclaimed in delight.

"I thought I'd surprise you," Connie smiled, stroking her hair like she was a child. "Uncle Fergus dropped me off. He's gone on another cruise."

Eilidh couldn't help but laugh. "Have you got a towel?"

"Of course. I hear there's a packed itinerary!"

"We certainly have!" Robyn grinned. "So we'd better get started."

First up was a trip to the pool for a few hours relaxation, then, a light lunch: a traditional Scottish menu, then an afternoon in the spa for a luxury Serenity massage and facial, to relax and rejuvenate.

"Och, this is the life!" Maudie exclaimed, as she sipped from her champagne glass. After a relaxing, lovely afternoon, they were all getting changed in their suite before heading down to dinner.

Eilidh smiled at her, admiring her. "It's helping me work up an appetite for tonight's dinner!"

Grace had book them all a three course meal, with the finest food Scotland had to offer, including an award winning chocolate and whisky pudding which Grace secretly wanted the recipe for.

Everyone nodded in agreement.

"I bet it'll make a change not to cook, eh, Gracie?" She said, as she glanced at Grace now.

"The dinner better be up to my standards, that's all I'm saying," she joked, and let out a contented sigh as she relaxed back against the pillows on her bed.

"Are you having a lovely time, Eilidh?" Nelly asked, and she nodded enthusiastically.

"I dinnae think I've had such a lovely hen do," she replied, her voice wobbling with emotion. "Sorry, I'm a bit emotional."

"You're bound to be emotional," Robyn replied. "Weddings are emotional events! Especially after a bad past experience. But rest assured, you have a good man, who adores you."

"Och, we knew that when you came back to Mossbrae," Enid replied. "He'd been in love with you for years."

Eilidh smiled despite her worries.

"Aye, Angus loves you!" Nelly cried. "He would never let you down."

"I know," Eilidh replied. "He's wonderful. He's so kind, and affectionate, and adores me... it's just, thinking about the wedding, and from what happened last time. It brings back bad memories...Especially after last time..."

Everyone turned to look at her, silently remembering Eilidh's previous wedding now which had ended in Eilidh being jilted by her cheating fiance who had run off with his ex-girlfriend.

"He wasnae the one for you," Nelly assured her.

"Aye, I know that now," she replied. "I'm so glad it didnae go ahead, knowing he was secretly in love with

Sophie. It wouldnae have worked. Especially as we lost Gran afore the wedding…"

She fell silent now, lost in the memory of that Christmas Eve, at the hotel they had chosen in Edinburgh for the reception, and remembered heading down to the ceremony room, her heart full of excitement, to find Jack's brother, Dan, waiting by the ceremony room.

"Dinnae panic, but there's no sign of Jack. We've all been waiting for over half an hour, and he hasnae turned up."

"He's not here?" Eilidh had cried. "Where is he?"

Dan had shaken his head. "We don't know. Has he contacted you?"

"No," Eilidh had replied, turning to Grace, and Grace would see she was trying not to panic. "Grace, can I have my mobile?"

Grace remembered handing Eilidh her phone, hating to see the pain in her eyes as she listened to the voicemail.

"He's cancelled the wedding…" Eilidh had cried, her voice cracking with emotion. "He's still in love with Sophie. He's left me for her!"

"Och, hen!" Connie cried, taking Eilidh in her arms. "Come on, let's get back upstairs. You dinnae need to face anyone. I'll come back down and handle everything for you."

"No, no, I need to explain the situation," Eilidh said, openly sobbing now. "Everyone has come all this way, and it's Christmas…I've left everyone down…"

Angus stepped forward and took her in his arms,

shushing her gently, as she sobbed, and Grace felt her heart break at the sight of it.

"Go with your Ma," he had said gently. "I'll take care of everything, and explain what's happening"

"Thank you," Eilidh had whispered, and allowed Connie to take her arm and lead her upstairs.

"We'll go and comfort Eilidh," Grace had announced, and followed Connie and Eilidh upstairs.

Grace would never forget walking up the stairs to the bridal suite, and pushing the door open to find Eilidh sobbing in Connie's arms on the bed.

"I should have realised," Eilidh had sobbed, as Connie shushed her. "They spent all their time together, even after we got engaged. He'd just asked me to marry him, and then he went out for a night out with Sophie and didnae come home until after midnight."

"Whisht, lass," Connie shushed her, rocking her like a child. "He should have been honest with you from the beginning, instead of letting it get this far…"

"I thought he loved me," Eilidh gasped. "I-I asked him if there was anything going on, and he denied it. He denied everything! He swore she was just a friend!"

"It'll be alright, hen," Grace murmured, stepping forward and pulling her into her arms. "He doesnae deserve you. What a cowardly thing to do, and on your wedding day of all days…"

"I thought he loved me," Eilidh repeated, sobbing, and Grace had rocked her, vowing she would never be put through this again.

~

"He's in the past now," Robyn piped up. She clinked her glass against hers, grinning. "Here's to the future."

"To the future!" Everyone cheered and clinked their glasses in a toast.

"Can you imagine how awful it would be if we married the first boyfriend we had?" Nelly chuckled.

"Aye," Enid agreed darkly. "You dinnae have doubts and if you do, they aren't for you."

"Remember that boy you went out with at vet college?" Grace chuckled.

"Boy sounds about right!" Robyn agreed darkly. "He wasnae mature enough to tie his shoelaces without help!"

"And he was training to be a vet?" Eilidh laughed.

"Aye," Robyn nodded. "I wasnae surprised he quit before the end of the first year."

"What about your old boyfriend? The one you met at culinary college?" Eilidh asked, turning to Grace now.

"Och! Do we need to speak about him?"

"What was his name?" Robyn piped up. "Archie?"

"Aye," Grace said coldly,

"Wasnae he the charming one who annoyed Da the one time you brought him home?"

"Did he?" Grace asked in surprise. "Da never said anything."

"He said he preferred Paul from the off set," Robyn replied conspiratorially.

"So did we," Maudie replied with a nod.

"You were destined for one another the moment you met," Enid intoned. "But you need to work hard to keep it that way."

Grace glanced at her now, feeling a sense of foreboding. Enid had a habit of making correct premonitions.

"What about me and Orion, Enid?" Robyn asked playfully.

"You'll have a surprise come your way, you just need patience."

Robyn smiled with satisfaction.

"What about you two? Can we expect a honeymoon baby?"

Eilidh blushed at the mischievous look in her eye, and thought about the pregnancy test she had in her bag, just in case.

"Och, there's plenty of time for all that!" She mumbled, feeling flustered.

"Are you two trying for a baby?" Grace asked excitedly, frowning at the champagne Robyn was sipping, then seeing the look on her face. "Sorry, that was insensitive."

Nelly put a hand on Robyn's arm. "It'll happen, hen."

"It already did…" Robyn murmured. "And all I have left of that is a scar and painful memories."

"Och, Robyn, I'm sorry," Grace cried, moving forward, and reaching for her sister but Robyn pulled away.

74

"And meanwhile, you have two healthy children you hardly get to spend time with because you're too busy with work. You dinnae know how lucky you are."

Grace opened her mouth to speak but remembering how she had asked Paul to take the kids to Eilidh's knowing he was busy because she wanted to get to the bakery, and knew in her heart Robyn was right. She had been missing out.

"It's no wonder things are strained with you and Paul. No wonder Enid is making premonitions."

"Robyn, I think you've had enough to drink," Grace said in her mum voice.

"I think you're right," Robyn conceded, standing up. "I'd better get an early night. I'm sorry Eilidh, I didnae mean to ruin your hen night…"

"Wait!" Grace almost shouted. "There's something you both need to see!"

Robyn paused in the doorway, to Grace's relief, and waited as Grace went to her bag and grabbed the cream, honeybee and thistle printed photo album.

"I think we need to remember why we're all here… To celebrate our friendship, and love for each other."

She sat back down on the bed heavily, and held it on her lap, handing it to Eilidh.

"Thats a beautiful album," Robyn admitted as she sat down on Eilidh's other side.

Eilidh opened it and gasped with delight as she flicked through the pages filled with photos of them as children, growing up together, and again with Robyn's wedding, as well as some of Eilidh and Angus together, capturing memories she had almost forgotten, over the years.

"Och, Gracie…How did you get these?" She asked in surprise, her eyes filling with tears.

"Da provided most of the ones of Angus and us as kids," Grace replied.

"I provided the rest," Connie replied, giving her hand a squeeze.

"This is such a wonderful present, thank you. I'm so lucky to have you all."

"And we are, you."

She turned to them now, wiping away a tear. "I want to thank you all for your support. I really needed it."

Connie reached for her hand and gave it a squeeze.

"We're always here for you, hen," Robyn assured her. "We've been friends for years. We aren't gonnae give up on you now."

Glancing at Grace, they exchanged a look, a silent apology the way sisters did, there was no need for words.

Then, she gently took the album from Eilidh, and placed it on the bed.

"Now, we're gonnae have a good night, and we're gonnae enjoy a wee drink and have a wonderful hen night. Because soon, we're gonnae have the wedding of the year, and you will get your happy ending," she added.

"I'll make sure of it," Grace affirmed, remembering her promise to Eilidh.

Chapter Six

 Week Later.

"And that," Eilidh said as she closed the hive, "ends our lesson today. Did you both enjoy it? Next time, we'll have a go at making candles."

Both kids let out a cheer as they headed inside to wash their hands and get changed out of their bee suits.

"Come on, let's get you home."

Angus had taken the Land Rover earlier that morning but was it only a twenty minute walk to the farm from the cottage, and as Eilidh breathed in the scent of roses by the door, it was already set to be a beautiful summer day.

As the kids skipped along the lane, chatting happily, Eilidh enjoyed the feeling of being out in the fresh air, listening to the bleating of the sheep, and the warmth of the sun on her skin, and soon, the farm came into view as they turned left up the farm track.

"Where is everyone?" Eilidh asked as they unlocked the gate, and walked through the main farmyard. It seemed strangely deserted, the dogs weren't rushing to greet them nor were the Runner Ducks rushing around, causing chaos. "Angus must be up the hillside," she said to herself, before catching the eye of the kids.

"What's tickled you two?" She asked, and Mhairi burst into fits of giggles.

"Come on, we've got a surprise for you!" Ollie called, taking her hand and tugging her along to the lower paddock.

"Surprise!" Grace yelled, unable to contain her own excitement. In the centre of the paddock was Angus, in shorts and a t-shirt, sitting on a dining chair, and Joe, Grace and Paul, Robyn and Orion, even The Trinity, were crowded around, holding flour, sugar, eggs, molasses, honey and treacle, and even what looked like a sack of feathers.

"Welcome to the Dooking," Grace grinned. "Come on, Eilidh, take a seat!"

"I thought I'd got out of it!" She laughed as she took a seat.

"It's tradition, hen, if you want this wedding to go without a hitch!" Maudie laughed.

Laughing, Eilidh took a seat, and turned to Angus, taking his hand.

"Ready?"

"As I'll ever be. I just hope all this washes off!"

"That's what the hosepipe is for, lad!" Joe called, brandishing the hosepipe for filling the water buckets. "The water's a wee bit cold but it's a nice warm day."

"Ah, this is gonnae be grand!"

"Three, two, one," Grace began the countdown, and took a step forward. "GO!"

Everyone advanced, throwing first the flour, then the treacle, eggs, sugar and molasses. Then the honey, and the other ingredients.

"You're gonnae both look braw once we're done!" Nelly cried, chuckling heartily as she threw feathers over them both

"Or a pair of chucks!" Eilidh replied. She glanced at Angus, who glanced back through the mess, grinning.

"I love you!" She called, standing up from the chair and taking the pillow from Maudie, throwing the feathers over him, laughing wildly.

"Och, you wee beastie!" Angus yelled, leaping off the chair and grabbing another pillow from Enid, throwing the feathers up in the air, so they fluttered like snow around them.

"Come here!" Angus called to Eilidh who had made it as far as the paddock gate.

"No chance!" She called back, breathless with laughter. "You smell like a compost heap!"

"Said she on the wedding night!" Orion cheered and Paul burst out laughing.

"That's why you love me!"

Angus ran after Eilidh, rugby tackling her to the

ground by the gate, rolling them both across the grass. Laughing hysterically, the pair of them hugged.

"I love you," Angus said, kissing her despite all the mess.

"I love you too," Eilidh replied. "Shall we get the others?"

"Aye, let's team up."

They got to their feet and raced after the kids, who were holding bags of jelly babies, who ran away shrieking with laughter.

"Retaliate!" Grace called, throwing more flour, and Robyn leapt in, throwing more eggs. Even Joe threw some more molasses, tears of laughter streaming down his sun weathered cheeks.

There was frenzied barking as Dash and Dram joined in, and then there was a flurry of quacking and squeaking as the Runner Ducks came charging across the yard.

"Get them, Dram!" Angus called, whistling.

"No! Dram, dinnae listen to Uncle Gus! You're no' to catch us!" Mhairi shrieked with joy.

Dram, paused, looking confused before racing back to Angus, barking wildly and flung himself at his master, rolling onto the ground as everyone burst out laughing.

They paused, panting from the exertion, and then joined the others in a messy group hug.

"You're gonnae have a wonderful wedding," Enid intoned, and Joe nodded.

"The best we've ever had in Mossbrae," Maudie announced, tears welling in her eyes.

"Wait, we've forgotten something!" Robyn cried, and rushed into the farmhouse, returning a few moments later with a bottle of champagne.

"To Eilidh and Angus!" She toasted, opening the bottle and spraying it all over the couple as everyone cheered and applauded.

"Here's to the Wedding of the Year!"

Chapter Seven

The air was filled with birdsong, the bleating of sheep, and the buzz of honeybees on the weekend of the wedding.

Eilidh stood in the doorway at Cairnmhor Farm, breathing in the scent of geraniums, and roses, and sighed with happiness. It was going to be a wonderful weekend and when she came home, she would be married. She could barely believe it herself. The excitement for the wedding day was palpable. Hair had been cut, wedding outfits had been brought, weekend bags were packed.

"Eilidh! The minibus is here!"

She turned at the sound of Grace's voice as she carried the wedding dress down the stairs. She had stayed here overnight with Grace, Robyn and the kids, as well as The Trinity, whilst Angus had stayed at the cottage with the rest of his groomsmen, Paul, Orion and Joe. They were all travelling together via hired minibus, and whilst it was a long journey to the Highlands, she was determined to enjoy every second of the journey.

"Well! I have to say it's a braw day for a wedding!" Grace announced as she carried the cake boxes out to the minibus, turning to Eilidh as she carried her dress in its protective case. "How are you feeling? Excited? Nervous?"

"Like I'm walking through a dream!" Eilidh smiled back, enjoying the cool summer breeze which was blowing in off the sea in the distance. "I hope we've got everything though…"

"Dinnae fret, as long as we've got you, the dress and the rings, that's all that matters. Without those three, the wedding can go ahead!" Robyn said as she brought her own dress out.

Soon, they had all the essentials loaded onto the bus.

"Come on, let's get you on that bus," Grace said, taking Eilidh's arm. "Remember now, right foot forward."

Eilidh glanced down at her feet.

"For luck."

Eilidh let out a nervous giggle, and with her right foot forward, boarded the bus.

"Here's the bride! Come and settle yourself, hen, plenty of room," Maudie announced, as she made her way out, dressed in a sunflower yellow dress. "We've all the snacks for the journey."

"What snacks do we have?" Ollie asked, and Maudie turned to him with a smile.

"Something verra special."

"I cannae wait to see the castle!" Mhairi cried, as she boarded the bus as Grace carried the kid's outfits out to the bus.

"It's no' a castle, hen, it's a mansion."

"Is Cousin Rory very rich?" Mhairi asked.

"He's done well for himself that's for sure," Enid said proudly. Rory had brought his estate, Capercaillie, a sixty acre estate in the Highlands near Fochabers, where he lived with a ten bedroomed mansion, orchards, and deer farm, and formal rose gardens.

"Come on, Ma!" Mhairi called, as she chose a seat on the bus. "We dinnae want to be late!"

"We're not gonnae be late, the wedding is tomorrow!" Ollie replied, following her, and Grace and Eilidh exchanged a glance, smiling at their enthusiasm.

It was lovely and cool on the bus, which was parked in the shade of the conifer trees as they waited for Angus and the rest of the party to join them as they were all travelling together.

Eilidh sat back, waiting, but her heart was racing with excitement, and she swore she could smell the scent of hyacinths around her, even though there were none out…

"Eilidh, hen,"

She jumped at the sound of her name to find Enid sitting behind her.

"Here," Enid murmured. "Open your hand."

She did, and Enid placed a silver sixpence into it.

"For your shoe. For luck."

"Thank you, Enid."

"Dinnae doubt it. Marianne is here with us," Enid said sagely. "She's coming along with us, and she cannot wait to see you and Angus wed."

Whilst none of The Trinity had ever professed to be clairvoyant, the accuracy of their premonitions made Eilidh trust Enid implicitly. If Marianne was here with them to enjoy the weekend, then she was, and Eilidh felt a wave of grief hit her, tears welling in her eyes.

Enid put an arm around her, smiling gently. "You have a wonderful future to look forward to."

"Really?"

"Aye, you need to believe it yourself."

"Can we crack open the drinks and snacks now?" Robyn asked loudly, breaking into her thoughts as she boarded the bus with two blue cool boxes, which she placed down by the front of the bus, and opened one up. "Ooh! I see you've packed all our favourites!"

"Robyn, hang on," Grace chided gently. "We havenae even set off yet. We need to wait for everyone to get here, and we have a long journey."

"Och, dinnae fret!" Robyn chided. "We've got two cool boxes and loads of food by the looks of it!"

Grace had packed her signature lemon and paprika roasted chicken thighs, smoked salmon quiche, ham lattice, and several bottles of homemade lemonade. "We still need to wait for the others…" Grace replied.

The car horn beeped as Angus's car pulled up and he and his groomsmen got out.

"Hello!" Angus greeted everyone as he helped Joe board the bus.

"Over here!" Maudie called, waving from her seat at the back of the bus where The Trinity had sat. Joe took a seat next to them, and settled himself near the welcoming breeze through the window as Maudie gave Mhairi some tablet, a caramelised fudge made with condensed milk and brown sugar.

"Yummy!" Mhairi enthused, as she took a bite. It was sweet, sugary and delicious.

"It will stop you feeling seasick too," said Maudie added with a smile.

"It'll be a smooth crossing," Enid intoned, as though to herself, and Grace nodded. If Enid said the crossing was going to be smooth, she believed her.

"Hello, Paddington," Angus murmured, taking a seat next to Eilidh at the front of the bus.

"Morning," she replied. "How are you feeling? I'm so nervous!"

"Och, you only have to promise to love me forever in front of all our family and friends," Angus grinned. "Dinnae fret, I'm nervous too."

"We'll help each other through," Eilidh promised, taking his hand and smiling at him. He was looking particularly gorgeous today, as he looked at her with those dark eyes. He was wearing a green polo shirt and jeans, dark hair ruffled.

"You look braw," Angus murmured, his gaze trailing across her orange sundress, long, light brown hair fastened into a neat topknot on top of her head.

Angus leant forward and tucked a stray hair behind her ear, and she beamed back.

"Och, would you look at that?" Maudie sighed with happiness as she settled herself. "I knew they were perfect for each other."

"A better match has yet to be beat," Enid replied, as a rare smile crossed her lips.

"Och, I dinnae think we've done too badly, aye?" Paul said, putting an arm around Grace. "How long has it been, Gracie?"

"A long time," Grace replied, with a warm smile. She turned her attention to her phone, checking for messages.

"Are you alright?" Paul murmured.

"Aye, I'm just checking my emails for more orders."

"Och, dinnae fret about that now," he replied. "I know. I just cannae help worrying about the bakery being closed for the weekend, with all those tourists I'm turning away."

He smiled, putting a gentle hand on top of hers. "This is your best friend's wedding weekend. Relax and enjoy it, no need to worry about work,"

Grace hesitated, and then put her phone back in her bag with a sigh. "Aye, you're right. It's been a busy few months."

"Aye. You need a break. You deserve it."

"Have some tablet, hen," Maudie said, leaning forward and offering her some.

"Thank you," Grace replied, and took some, enjoying it's sweetness and how much it reminded her of her childhood. "I used to make this with Ma," she murmured.

"Aye, Annabelle used to wonderful at making tablet."

Grace nodded silently, feeling a wave of grief for her late mother.

"It's alright, hen," Paul said, putting an arm around her, rubbing her shoulder gently. "It's gonnae be a wonderful weekend."

"Are we all ready?" Angus asked, his voice raised above the chatter. "Shall we set off before we miss the ferry?"

His answer was a round of whoops and cheers as the driver started the engine, and they set off towards the harbour.

"Let's get this party started!" Robyn cried, grabbing a bottle of home made lemonade. "Shall we crack these open?"

She opened one of the bottles of lemonade, and poured out plastic cup fills, handing them out.

Grace was about to chide her little sister but then, she remembered what Paul had said, and accepted a cup as Robyn handed one to her.

"To Angus and Eilidh!" Robyn toasted. "Here's to a wonderful wedding weekend!"

"To a wonderful wedding weekend!" Everyone cheered. "To Angus and Eilidh!"

Chapter Eight

*A*fter a smooth crossing as Enid predicted, the party made their way towards the Highlands.

As The Trinity lead them in another rousing version of Mairi's Wedding, (changed to Eilidh for the occasion,) they drove further into the Highlands. The children provided the percussion, tapping on the empty Tupperware boxes whilst everyone else clapped along.

"We ought to ask Rory to play this at the ceilidh tonight," Eilidh suggested, turning to Angus, who nodded enthusiastically. "This is lovely. Especially the food!"

"Is there any left?" Angus laughed.

The cool boxes, were now half full, and the cool summer breeze, scented with conifers blew through the open bus windows as they drove.

· · ·

Enid glanced out of the window, and a light frown came across her face at the clouds gathering in the distance, despite the hot summer's day.

"Och, we need to be careful, there's trouble ahead... So foul and fair a day I have not seen..."

"Trouble?" Grace replied. "What kind of trouble?"

Enid turned to her, staring at her, her eyes serious. "In order to face the future, we must sometimes face our past..."

"Face the past?" Grace asked in alarm, and Paul put his arm around her.

"Aye, we're facing our past, heading back to where we got engaged, remember?" He dropped a kiss on the side of her temple. "Dinnae fret."

Grace nodded, but she couldn't help feeling rattled that something was afoot.

It was almost lunchtime by the time they reached Rory's estate, Capercaillie, and everyone felt a thrill of excitement as they drove through the main gates and onto the estate.

"Here we are!" Mhairi and Ollie squealed with excitement, as the bus drove up a long gravelled driveway flanked with conifer trees, and in the distance, they could see the conifer forests and rugged mountainous terrain.

"I forget how amazing this is!" Grace gasped at the sight of the honey-coloured stone Georgian mansion house, which stood at the head of the driveway. As they drove up the driveway and parked outside, they saw that Rory and Isla were waiting for them, with baby William, who was now six months old.

"Hello!" Angus and Eilidh greeted them warmly as they got off the bus. "Haven't you grown?!"

"Aye, he's a braw, strong lad now," Isla said, as she handed William over to Eilidh, and he giggled in her arms.

"I cannae believe how much he's grown!" Eilidh gasped, turning to Robyn now, who had also helped deliver baby William when he made an early appearance when Rory and Isla had visited at Christmas, in the middle of a snowstorm.

William, with his chubby cherubic cheeks, red hair and blue eyes, gave her a toothy smile as Eilidh handed him to Robyn for a cuddle, and he burst into peals of laughter as she tickled him.

"Aye, it's gone so fast! And now you two are getting married tomorrow," Rory grinned.

"I couldn't think of a more wonderful place to get married," Eilidh sighed with happiness.

"I couldnae agree more," Paul said, putting an arm around Grace's shoulders. "It brings back fond memories, aye?"

"Aye, it does," Grace smiled, looking up at him. He looked so handsome in the early afternoon sunlight, with his red hair, bright blue eyes, and broad, handsome face. His arm around her was reassuring and safe, and for a moment, she allowed herself to relax.

"Come on in," Rory said after he helped get their

cases out of the back of the minibus. "Let's get you all settled in, and then we can have a tour of the estate?"

"I've always wanted to see the estate, it's been years," Nelly sighed with happiness.

"That sounds braw!" Grace announced, as she carried the cake boxes, and followed everyone else inside as they gently crunched across the gravel.

The echo of her footsteps clicked on the black and white chequered hallway floor as the party entered the house. Glancing up, she admired the chandelier which sat overhead, tiny rainbows of light dancing around the hallway, bouncing off the heritage-blue walls, Georgian panelling, and the resin deer heads on the walls.

"I'll show you to your rooms," Rory said, as he lead everyone upstairs. "This way."

Grace took in the paintings lining the walls as they ascended the stairs, until her eyes fell upon the magnificent painting of the stag at the top of the stairs, and her eyes widened. "Is that a Landseer? The Monarch of the Glen?"

"Aye, it is," Rory said proudly. "At least, it's meant to be. It's a copy, done by our good friend, Flora."

"It's magnificent!" Grace replied as she admired it for a moment. The detail was so accurate, she could have sworn it was the original. "I thought it was the original."

"Aye, everyone thinks that," Rory grinned, as he lead them along a long hallway to the bedrooms.

Grace hesitated a moment longer and then followed everyone.

"Here we are," Rory said to Eilidh and Angus, as he opened a door on his right, "Our Bridal Suite."

"This is wonderful!" Eilidh gasped. The room smelt of roses and geraniums, and fresh laundry. She glanced at the heritage pink paint on the walls, which matched the floral bed linen on the super king bed, then across at the chaise longe by the bay window, from which there was a beautiful view of the hillside and conifer forests and she gasped in delight.

"Look at that view!"

"You can see Golden Eagles first thing on a morning," Rory replied. "We have nesting pairs in the forest."

"Really?" she asked as she admired the view.

"Can we see our room?" Mhairi begged, tugging at Grace's sleeve. "Have we got Golden Eagles too?"

"You've got a view of the deer," Rory announced, taking her hand, and led her out of the room, to the one a few doors down. He opened the door to a more modest but equally lovely room which gave a gorgeous view of the rest of the estate. Glancing out of the window, Mhairi and Ollie could see the road leading down through the estate, towards the formal rose garden, and the deer park.

"Can we go and have our tour yet?" Ollie asked.

"Aye, we're all going in a moment," Grace replied, sniffling a yawn.

"You can stay here and have a rest if you need to," Paul murmured. "I can look after the kids."

"I'm alright, I can do with the fresh air," Grace insisted. She picked up her phone, checking for the signal.

"You'll get a better signal outside," Rory answered her. "Up here the signal is a bit ropey."

"That's one thing less to worry about this weekend," Paul replied easily. "Then you can properly relax."

Grace nodded, but silently, wondered if she was going to be able to, given there was still so much to do before tomorrow.

There was a delighted shriek from behind them, and they all hurried out to see what the noise was.

"I cannae believe the size of this en suite!" Maudie, her candy floss pink hair dancing around her shoulders. "I could live here! Have you room for us three?"

"Aye, of course we have," Rory smiled. "You're most welcome to move in any time. Shall we head off on our tour?"

Chapter Nine

"First, we'll see the orchards," Rory announced, as they all set off, enjoying the view as the minibus weaved its way, zigzagging down the drive leading from the house to the rest of the estate.

He parked the minibus, and they departed, following him, chattering excitedly, as they walked through the wrought iron gates of the walled orchard, and were enveloped in the heady scent of apple blossom, and the sight of grand apple trees lining the path.

Mhairi ran on ahead, discreetly picking an apple from a low hanging branch, and took a bite before anyone noticed.

"Och! It's bitter!" She cried, giving herself away, and Grace turned to her in alarm.

"I'm sorry," Mhairi replied, dropping the apple. "I thought it would be sweet."

"They are cooking apples," Rory grinned. "If you want to find an eating apple, they're over here."

"May I have one?"

"Aye, of course," Rory replied, handing her a shiny red apple, and she took a grateful bite.

"We grow eating and cooking apples," he explained. "We make our own cider too."

"Can we have an orchard?" Angus asked Eilidh with a grin.

"Mind yourselves," Rory added as they walked through to the next part of the garden. "We keep the bees in this section."

"I'm glad to see they're settling in alright," Eilidh said happily. Last Spring, she had sent Rory a hive and Queen, along with a nuc to help him pollinate the apple trees. Now, he had three hives and was doing well as a new beekeeper.

The hives were fenced in by a small white wooden fence in one corner of the orchard. "Aye. They've settled in well, and they love the apple blossom. Helps with the cider making. You can all try some of the cider later. Apple juice for the kids, of course."

"That sounds grand with this hot weather!" Angus agreed.

"We're training to be beekeepers," Mhairi piped up proudly. "Aunty Eilidh has been teaching us."

"Is that so? Well, you've got a grand teacher there. I bet you're going to be wonderful beekeepers," Rory replied.

"They've taken to it like a duck to water," Eilidh said proudly, smiling at Grace.

"Ah, in that case, you could both come and work for me once you've learnt it all."

"Yes! We'd love to!" Mhairi replied. "We've even got our own bee suits!"

"Can we have a beekeeping lesson here?" Ollie asked.

"Not this weekend!" Mhairi chipped in. "We're bridesmaids for Aunty Eilidh."

"I'm a page boy, not a bridesmaid!" Ollie laughed, and Mhairi's face fell, bottom lip wobbling, and sensing the kids were on the brink of an argument, Grace took her hand.

"Shall we see the rose gardens?"

"The rose gardens are this way," Rory called, and they allowed followed him, admiring the trees as they walked, enjoying the shade they provided as the day seemed to have got even hotter.

"Come on," Paul murmured in her ear, taking her hand in his, and she realised it had been ages since they had even as much as held hands as they walked through to the rose garden. The garden was a huge arch, covered in roses, and several bushes lined the gravel covered paths on both sides. The scent was almost overwhelming, and the scent brought Grace back to that wonderful night, the night Paul had proposed.

"I think it was this very spot, aye?" Paul asked, pausing for a moment and glancing at her. "Where I asked you to be my wife?"

"You remember the spot you knelt down?" Grace laughed at how well he remembered that tiny detail. For a moment, enjoying the memory of that night, the night of Isla and Rory's wedding, when he had suggested a walk in the darkened rose gardens, which had been lit with tea lights, giving it a romantic ethereal glow, the best night of her life.

Glancing at him now, so many years later, it felt like a lifetime ago, and catching her eye, Paul smiled back at her, and their gaze met for a long moment, making her feel like time had stopped still.

"Och, look at that look," Nelly sighed. "You could strike a match between them!"

Mhairi burst into giggles.

"Of course," Paul murmured, pulling her close. "How could I forget?"

"Och, it's so romantic!" Maudie gasped to Nelly as she watched them. "There's nothing so lovely as two people in love."

"And to still be in love all this time later."

"We should go," Grace said softly, looking up at him and meeting his gaze now. She glanced up and saw their were clouds gathering in the distance. "The weather looks like it's taking a turn…"

"Still worrying about what Enid said?" Paul asked. "Och, dinnae fret. You cannae control the weather."

"Ma!" Mhairi called. "Da! Come on!"

"Come on," Paul relented. "We'd better go."

∽

"We'll head down to see the deer now," Rory announced, turning right, and then they headed down the hill, breathing in the scent of conifer and the drifting scent of roses from behind them.

"The paddock stretches all the way down the hill," Rory explained. "We currently have over a hundred does and five stags. We keep the hinds and calves in this section, and the stags in the other end. They like to be separate until it's the rut in October. We then pair one stag to twenty hinds. It gives them all a mini harem and reduces the risk of fighting."

"Aye, sounds fair to me," Orion joked.

"Are there many babies?" Mhairi asked.

"We've got about ninety calves," Rory replied. "They're a little bit bigger now though."

"They're over there!" Ollie said in a hushed tone. "Look!"

They kept walking down the hillside, until the herd came into view. They were wonderful creatures, Eilidh thought as they got closer. "Look at their coats!"

Their coats were gleaming, red brown in the afternoon sunlight, and everyone agreed in hushed murmurs, that they were the most magnificent animals they had ever seen.

"They look wonderful," Robyn sighed, adding, ever the vet. "All in great health."

"Aye, and the calves are too. You cannae see them in the long grass, but you might get a glance of them," Rory added, his voice proud.

"Here with the deer would make for some brilliant wedding photos," Enid said, glancing at Eilidh.

"That's a brilliant idea," Eilidh said to Angus who smiled, and gave each other a look which made all the women swoon.

"Aye, it would," Angus said, absently, making Eilidh turn to him with a frown.

"Are you alright?"

"Shall we head on to the estate shop for a refreshing drink?" Rory suggested.

Everyone agreed it sounded wonderful and they walked back across the path, towards the farm shop. It was a smaller version of the Georgian mansion, and inside it was lovely and cool from the summer heat.

"We've been making cider since we first came to Capercaillie," Rory explained as he opened a bottle, and poured the dark amber coloured liquid into glasses for the adults and apple juice for the children. "It was trial and error, but I think we've finally got that sweet, slightly tart balance just right with this one. But before we enjoy it, let's have a wee toast. Slante! To Eilidh and Angus. The Happy Couple!"

"The happy couple!" Everyone cheered, clinking their glasses together and taking a grateful sip. The cider was exactly as Rory promised, a sweet, mellow taste, with a sharp, robust aftertaste which was delightful.

"This is wonderful," Grace agreed, allowing herself to relax for a moment as she sipped the cider.

"Let's show you around," Rory said and for the next half an hour, they enjoyed looking around the shop, at the homemade honey, the homemade cider, and the paintings on the walls of rural life which reminded Joe fondly of the old days. It was dark and cool in here, a relief from the summer heat, and Grace wished she had brought her purse with her when she saw a variety of honey, cider, and apple juice she wanted to buy.

When the tour was finished, they headed out and back to the bus, and saw the sun was now seeking shelter behind the gathering clouds.

Grace looked up and felt an uncomfortable churn of foreboding she couldn't blame on the cider. She glanced back to tell Paul to see he was joking with Orion, (between them they had finished the cider and were getting quite merry.)

As though to confirm Enid's premonition, the sky went dark, and the heavens opened as torrential rain fell, until it was falling so hard it was bouncing off the ground.

"We'd better get back to the bus!" Rory announced loudly, unfazed. "We dinnae want to be soaked for the ceilidh tonight!"

They all hurried back to the bus and found their seats, but Grace was feeling decidedly jangled.

"Enid said there was trouble afoot…" she murmured in alarm, glancing across at Eilidh and Angus, who were deep in conversation.

"Angus!" she hissed, nudging him.

"What? Sorry, I was miles away," he replied apologetically.

"No' getting cold feet are you?" Eilidh asked with light concern.

"No, of course not!" He exclaimed, reaching for her hand and squeezing it reassuringly, lowering his voice. "Dinnae laugh, but I was reciting my vows. I want to make sure I dinnae slip up tomorrow."

"I dinnae care if you do," Eilidh said, stroking his cheek. "I would know you mean every word."

"There's something else too," he added as they took their seats.

Eilidh's face fell a little. "What?"

"Well... We've got some more guests coming. Actually, they've invited themselves."

"Aye?" Eilidh asked, unfazed. "Who?"

"Brace yourself," Angus dropped his voice to a whisper. "Uncle Cedric, and Aunty Odette."

Her eyes widened with alarm, and she glanced over her shoulder at The Trinity who were chatted animatedly with Mhairi and Ollie. "Is that no' gonnae cause a kerfuffle?"

"Dinnae fret, I'm sure they aren't gonnae make a scene. They aren't gonnae be here until tomorrow, the day of the ceremony."

"Are you two whispering sweet nothings to each other?" Grace teased. Seeing their faces, she frowned. "What's going on?"

"Cedric and Odette are coming," Eilidh replied in a hushed whisper.

Grace visibly paled. "Are you serious?"

She turned to Rory.

"Aye. Cedric was verra insistent," Rory replied apologetically.

"Oh, Jings!" Grace cried, and then turned it into a coughing fit.

"Are you alright, hen?" Maudie called from the back of the bus, where The Trinity and Joe were sitting.

"Aye!" Grace called, nodding vigorously. "Crumb gone down the wrong way!"

She turned back to Angus and Eilidh. "Enid said trouble is afoot. We cannot tell The Trinity!"

"What's happening?" Robyn asked, who was sitting behind them. She leant forward, keen to hear all the gossip.

"Cedric and Odette are joining us."

"Odin's Other Eye is coming? Oh, Jings!" Robyn hissed.

"Dinnae call her that, it's a horrible nickname."

"I never gave her it. But it's accurate, she knows everything. She's like the evil fourth member of The Trinity."

"Robyn, will you behave!" Grace hissed, in her best Mum voice.

"I'm sure she didnae mean them though," Robyn carried on. "I hope there's no' too much trouble when The Trinity find out…"

"There willnae be any trouble," Grace assured them both as Enid's words rang in her head. "I'll make sure of it."

Chapter Ten

*T*he ceilidh began at six, and was held in the dining hall, which was a huge room, filled with Georgian panelling, a hardwood floor, and wide windows along the far end of the room, offering more glorious panoramic views of the estate. Even in the twilight, it was beautiful, as the summer evening sunlight danced across the scene.

The sound of whooping and cheering filled the hall as the music from the ceilidh filled with the house. In the dining room, the live ceilidh band was playing a lively jig, and Grace watched with delight as Eilidh and Angus took to the dance floor, twirling each other around in a circle, laughing uproariously.

"Och, they're a braw couple," Maudie said, wiping an eye.

"Aye, they do," Grace said.

"It's a shame Marianne isnae here to see it," Nelly

added, shaking her head sadly. "She'd have been so very proud."

Grace nodded, and felt herself getting choked up with emotion.

"And it's all thanks to us, eh, lass?" Maudie grinned mischievously. "If it wasnae for our interfering-"

"Matchmaking," Grace corrected her, and Maudie began chuckling heartily.

"Och, it was destined that they would be together," Enid intoned, eating a piece of smoked salmon quiche. "Ever since they were wee, you could see they belonged together."

Grace and the Trinity admired them now, feeling emotion welling up at the sight of how in love Eilidh and Angus were.

"Can you imagine how bonny the bairns will be?" Maudie gasped.

"Aye, they'd be gorgeous," Nelly and Grace agreed.

"What's this?" Robyn asked, walking over with a full plate of buffet food. "This quiche is braw! Almost as yummy as yours."

"We're just admiring the happy couple," said Grace. "And giving ourselves a clap on the back for our superb matchmaking skills!"

"Aye?" Robyn grinned, finishing her quiche. "We did a grand job if I dinnae say so myself."

She sat down on a faded armchair beside the Trinity and Grace, balancing her plate on her lap.

"Och, is that your second plate?" Grace asked in surprise.

"Aye, it is, why?" Robyn asked, raising an eyebrow.

"Nothing," Grace replied. "I didnae know you liked vegetarian quiche… no' eating the smoked salmon?"

Robyn shook her head. "It's no' as braw as yours… speaking of which I cannae wait to try that cake tomorrow."

Grace took another bite of another paprika roast chicken drumstick, and sighed with pleasure.

"This is almost as good as your's!" Robyn said, taking another bite, and she frowned lightly. "You must get the recipe!"

"Aye, I wonder who is doing the catering?" Grace replied. It was a delicious spread, she thought, admiring the table now, at the canapés, venison pies, smoked salmon quiche, and Cranachan over on the pudding table.

"Rory!" Robyn called over, waving him over.

Grace winced, "Robyn, dinnae shout across the room…"

"Everything alright? Having a good time?" Rory asked, holding a plateful of buffet food himself. He had changed into his family Gordon tartan and a dark navy jacket and dress shirt, closely cropped blond hair slicked back off his face, making him look younger than his forty-three years.

"We were wondering who's doing the catering for the wedding? This spread is delicious!" Robyn said enthusiastically.

"Ah," Rory said, looking a little awkwardly. "My friend…"

"Bide my words," Enid said aloud, as though to herself. "Something wicked this way comes..."

"I didnae know Enid knew Shakespeare," Robyn murmured, but Grace shook her head, glancing across at Enid now.

"Something wicked?"

Enid nodded and headed back towards the buffet table.

"Fancy a dance?" a voice called in her ear and she turned to see Paul, dressed in his own family tartan, smiling at her. He held out a hand, then dropped it, frowning. "Are you alright?"

Grace shook her head and sighed. "I'm thinking about what Enid said...What does she mean by something wicked and trouble brewing?"

"Och, are you still letting that worry you? Come and dance, take your mind off things."

He reached for her hand, and Grace was about to take it when she remembered.

"Och Jings! I've forgotten the cake! I need to put the cake away, to assemble it tomorrow."

She leant forward and kissed his cheek. "I'll be right back."

She hurried over to Rory and explained the situation, and he pointed her in the direction of the kitchens.

"Rhona should be around, she'll give you a hand."

Grace thanked him and hurried upstairs to grab the cake boxes which she had left in the cool of the en-suite of their bedroom, then slowly carried it downstairs towards the kitchens.

· · ·

"Are you alright, hen?" Asked a voice and Grace peeked around the boxes to see Rhona, Rory and Isla's housekeeper coming towards her.

"Rhona!" She cried in delight. "It's been years! How are you?"

"Still here," she said, as she took the top box from her, and Grace took her in more closely. The older woman was in her sixties, dressed in a blue and white floral dress, her oyster blonde hair weaved discreetly with silver, giving her an ethereal look. "It's lovely to see you, and I hear you've brought the weans. I havnae seen them for years."

"Aye, they're five and seven now," Grace said proudly.

"Already? How time flies!"

"How are you?"

"Och, getting on with things," Rhona said gently. "I'm on my own now that Leonard is no longer with us…"

"Leonard?" Grace asked in alarm. "Has he…"

"Och, no. We aren't seeing each other any more."

Grace couldn't help but smile at this. "I'm sorry to hear that."

Rhona gave a light shrug so Grace decided to move the conversation on.

"How are Leanna and Jo?" She asked and Rhona's face lit up at the sound of her granddaughter's names. They were small children the last time Grace had seen them, but now were in their twenties.

"Ah, Leanna's here somewhere. She helps me with

the housekeeping whilst she's off from catering college. She wants to be a baker too, and Jo is with her aunt and uncle over in Braerannoch. She's just graduated from vet school."

Braerannoch was a coastal town a few miles from here, which was popular with tourists and had an annual flower festival.

"Ah, that's wonderful! Robyn will be pleased to hear that. Braerannoch is a lovely place."

"How is Robyn? I must come and catch up with you all. I've lost touch with a lot of folk sadly, since Gregor passed..."

"Come to the ceilidh," Grace suggested, but Rhona shook her head.

"Ah, I said I'd help Rory out until it was over."

"He willnae mind one dance."

"Alright then," Rhona relented. "Let's go and put these away first."

They walked down the maze of corridors, the music from the ceilidh fading the further they walked until they reached the kitchens. Rhona pushed the door open and Grace was hit with the welcoming coolness.

"We can put them over here, hen, ready to assemble tomorrow."

"Thank you," Grace replied, as they walked past the huge work top in the centre of the room, with a grand open fireplace which had once housed a spit for roasting meat, and walls lined with copper pans, like one of those owned by the National Trust for Scotland or Scottish Heritage, and cream Aga in the corner of the room.

They opened the cupboard, and Rhona grabbed a stool to reach the top shelves where they put the cake boxes.

"Rhona? Have you seen the list for tomorrow?" a familiar voice called and Grace froze, almost dropping the last cake box. It couldn't be. This couldn't be what Enid at meant.. She'd recognise that voice anywhere…

She turned to see the man in the doorway, dressed in a red, green and gold tartan she recognised.

"It's here," Rhona replied, handing over the list. "Ah, Grace, this is Archie."

Shit, he was *that* Archie. Her ex boyfriend. Archie bloody Lennox, Grace thought as they greeted each other politely. His gaze meeting hers, and she felt like she had gone back in time twenty years. His hawkish features, bright blue eyes, tousled dark hair, and the sharpest cheekbones she had ever seen were so familiar. Seeing him now, Grace winced. They had dated briefly in her catering days, and he'd spent most of that lying to her and messing around with other women, breaking her heart over and over again. He was the last person she had wanted to see again, let alone this weekend.

"Archie is the head of the catering team this weekend, and he's doing the food for the wedding," Rhona explained, turning to Archie. "Grace is doing the cake."

Grace climbed the step and put the last cake box into the cupboard, and brushed her hands across her emerald green tea dress she was wearing for the ceilidh, and tucked a stray hair behind her ear self consciously.

"Right, hen," Rhona announced. "I'll leave you to it. See you back at the ceilidh."

"Dinnae forget to come and have a dance."

Grace and Archie watched her go, and then Grace pulled her attention back to him, realising she was going to have to at least be polite to him.

"It's good to see you again," he said in his clipped English accent, and she forced herself to meet his gaze. However, when she did, she was immediately transported back to their dating days, as Enid's words about facing her past rang in her ears.

He hadn't changed in twenty years. She let out a breath she realised she had been holding, as Enid's words rang in her head about facing her past and wondered what it meant for this weekend. She let out her breath, trying to ignore that memory of their first meeting, all those years ago…

Chapter Eleven

he Past.

Winter. Aviemore.

"Are you coming home for Christmas?" Annabelle asked as Grace rang home that weekend. Christmas was weeks away, but Grace didn't have to think twice.

"Of course I am!" Grace replied. "I wouldnae miss you or Da's anniversary for the world! I'll prepare the buffet if you want."

"Aye, that sounds like a good idea," Annabelle replied brightly.

"I'll be home on the 23rd," Grace replied and hung up.

"Thats grand," Annabelle replied. "Robyn is coming

home on the 23rd too, so I'll see you both then. Take care."

"Aye, I will. See you then. I have to go, I'm running late."

"See you soon."

Annabelle hung up and went to check the lamb stew, loving the scent of rosemary and garlic as it drifted around the kitchen. It would soon be Christmas, and there was still a lot to do.

Glancing out of the living room window, she looked out at the heavy clouds gathering in the west, bringing the threat of snow with it. That was the thing about this time of year, the unpredictability of the weather, and Christmas was the busiest time of year on the farm. She looked at the snow covered hills and in the distance she could see the quad bike, moving along and gathering the pregnant ewes to get them into the lambing barn.

The sudden pain in her side made her cry out, dropping the spoon on the floor with a clatter. That had been the third time this week… if it carried on, she'd have to get it checked out, she thought to herself. But glancing around the kitchen now, at the boots by the door, coats hanging up on the coat rack, and the crackle of the log burner in the living room, there was so much to do still before she even felt ready for Christmas…

· · ·

Turning away from the window, trying to ignore the pain in her side as she grabbed some painkillers from the cupboard, trying to refocus her mind. There was too much to do, and the first thing was to plan their wedding anniversary party, and then, she needed to find the Christmas decorations.

It was time to get Christmassy…

Grace hung up the phone and hurried down the corridor. Damn it she was going to be late, and their tutor, Giles, was not going to be pleased. This was her first term at catering college, and Grace had made an extra special effort to be early every day, but today she had blotted her copy book.

"I'm so sorry I'm late! I was calling my mother, making plans for Christmas."

All the other students turned at the sound of her voice, as she stood in the doorway, red faced and panting with exertion.

"Aye, that's all well and good, but try to be here in time," Giles said, turning back to the rest of the students. "Right, now you all know the basics, we're gonnae move on. By the end of term, we're gonnae be learning how to make a croquembouche. Let's head to the main table."

Grace followed, feeling like she was applying for Masterchef.

"I have to say you know how to make an entrance,"

Archie, one of her colleges, asked, and she turned to him, admiring his tall, broad frame, feeling her cheeks burn as her heart raced. He was a couple of years older than her, English, and she could tell that from the way he smiled at her, with those hawkish blue eyes, closely cropped dark hair, and his sharp, elegant cheekbones, he was *trouble*.

"Thanks."

She had had crushes before but she felt for the first time, that she was falling for him hard. "Have you made plans for the holidays yet?"

"I was thinking of staying in Aviemore," Archie replied casually. "Heard you're heading home. Is it far?"

"Mossbrae, it's in the Inner Hebrides," Grace replied.

"Sounds nice," Archie replied. "I've never been to the Inner Hebrides. I've heard there's a lot of farms there."

"Aye, I live on one of them," Grace replied proudly. "A sheep farm."

"Is that so? So you didnae want to go into farming?"

"No," Grace replied. "I've always loved cooking. What about you?"

"You two love birds stop chatting and get over here. Arrange a date and then we can get on!" Giles interrupted.

Grace flushed to the roots of her hair, and Archie gave her another lazy smile.

"Well, sounds like a good idea. What do you think?"

"Aye, that would be lovely," she replied, feeling her heart hammering.

"Tomorrow afternoon? We could go to the cinema," Archie replied. "There's that new action film on."

"Aye. I'd love that."

"Great. I'll meet you at the cinema at six pm, after work."

The afternoon's task was to make cinnamon swirls, a recipe Grace knew backwards and soon, the scent of cinnamon and nutmeg brought back memories of weekend baking with Annabelle and she felt a clutch of homesickness.

"Right," Giles announced, as he checked everyone's at the end of the lesson, and Grace felt like she was a contestant on Great British Bake Off, facing Paul Hollywood. Come to think of it, Giles looked a bit like him…

"Those are very good," he said, admiring them. The cinnamon rolls were filled with raisins and apple, and the scent reminded Grace of baking on cold rainy days during the school holidays. "You've got the makings of a good chef. Well done."

"Thank you, Chef."

Grace felt the grin spread across her face as everyone applauded.

"Well done," Archie murmured as everyone departed to change out of their whites, leaving just them two behind. "You can make me some next time."

"Sure." Grace smiled back at him, blushing.

"See you tomorrow."

"Aye," she murmured back, feeling like she was in a dream. "See you tomorrow."

It was almost six by the time Grace reached the cinema, and she let out a long breath as she saw Archie waiting for. He was wearing a navy shirt, and jeans under his leather jacket, his hair slicked back and she noticed he was clean shaven, highlighting those wonderful cheekbones as he smiled at her.

"Hello," he said warmly, his breath coming out in a plume of steam in the icy December air. "You look lovely."

"Thank you," she said shyly, glancing down at her own outfit, a peridot green floral shirt dress and dark brown knee boots under a black wool coat.

"Shall we go in?" Archie asked, offering his arm and nodding, she took it, and they headed into the cinema.

"That was a lovely film. I ought to head back, we have to be up early," Grace said as they left, checking her watch.

"You want to wrap it up this early?" Archie asked in surprise. "I had a surprise for you."

"Really? What did you have in mind?"

"You'll see," Archie grinned back, and flagged them a taxi.

Archie lived in a Georgian apartment in the centre of Aviemore, and Grace liked it on sight, with it's high vaulted ceilings and hardwood floors. The kitchen was something else, an entire row of drawers and cupboards lined one wall, and in centre stood an antique cream Aga. It was her dream kitchen and she felt her hear race with excitement at the sight of the dining table set for two.

"Have a seat. I'm going to cook for you," Archie said pulling out a chair.

"What are we eating?"

"Ah, it's a family recipe, a speciality of mine," he said, getting Tupperware boxes out of a nearby fridge. Grace saw paprika and lemon roast chicken thighs, tomatoes, a crusty baguette, and a bottle of white wine. "Is this enough?"

"Och, it's more than enough!" Grace exclaimed as he opened the wine and poured her a glass, clinking it against hers.

He handed her the Tupperware box containing the chicken thighs. "Try these. I've been practicing the recipe."

Grace tried one and was blown away as her mouth was invited to a mix of spicy, sweet and delicious flavours. "Och! This is braw, Archie."

119

"I was just experimenting, really," Archie said with a shrug. "I can give you the recipe if you like."

"So, we've established you can cook, what else do you like to do?" She asked as she bit into a tomato.

"I like reading," Archie replied. "I used to read a lot as a kid, but recently I've got out of the habit, and I'd love to get into it again. How about you?"

"Growing up on a farm, I love being around nature, but I dinnae want to be a farmer,. I do love the country-side though," Grace replied.

"I'm afraid I'm a City boy myself," Archie said, his gaze was fixed on her. "But that sounds idyllic."

"Aye, it was lovely. Just no' so much in the winter months with all the mud and rain."

"Oh, we live in Scotland, that part of the deal, isn't it?" Archie joked. "A bit of mud and rain."

"What made you want to get into cooking?"

"My dad is a chef, so I thought I'd give it a go," Archie joked, which made her laugh at his honesty. "What about you?"

"I've always loved cooking, even more than farm-ing. I used to cook with my Ma when I was young, and it seemed inevitable I would go to culinary college. I want to own a bakery and make my own cakes."

Archie looked impressed. "Really? That sounds bril-liant. What will you call it?"

"Something to do with ducks, I think," Grace replied. "I love ducks."

"Ducks?" He asked with a bemused smile.

"I grew up on a farm."

"Yes. You said. That's wonderful, to have a dream like that, and to make it happen."

"Aye, I suppose it is," Grace replied as she ate another tomato. "Do you remember me saying I was heading home for Christmas?"

"Yes. I remember."

"I was wondering, would you like to come with me? It's my parent's wedding anniversary. They've been married for twenty years. I'm doing the catering."

"Thats amazing," Archie replied as he poured them another glass of wine. "So you want me to meet your parents? A bit sudden for a first date, don't you think?"

"Och, I didnae mean it like that!" Grace gasped and Archie chuckled softly.

"I'm just kidding. I'd like to come with you."

"Really?"

"Of course. I really like you, Grace."

"I like you too."

With that, Archie leant forward and kissed her.

"Oh," Grace murmured, and kissed him again, wrapping his arms around his neck, and then he took her hand and lead her upstairs to finish their date.

Chapter Twelve

resent Day.

"Grace?"

Grace jumped at the sound of her name, as Paul appeared in the doorway.

He glanced between Archie and Grace, and his face darkened before he turned back to Grace. "Have you managed to sort the cake?"

"Aye. I have," Grace replied, moving towards him.

"Well, Archie, this is a surprise," Paul said, staring hard at Archie now, how stared back at him impassively.

"Yes, I suppose it is. I'm heading the catering team this weekend for the wedding."

"We should get back," Grace said, placing a hand on Paul's chest to move him forwards. "Come on."

"See you soon," Archie said to their retreating backs.

. . .

"Why didnae you say your ex-boyfriend was gonnae be here?" Paul hissed as they made their way back along the corridors and the sound of the ceilidh got louder, much to Grace's relief.

"I didnae know he was gonnae be here," Grace said reasonably, turning to face him.

Paul looked unconvinced, so she reached for his hand. "Paul, maybe this is what Enid was talking about, that I need to face my past in order to look to the future."

"And there I was, thinking it meant our past. Not your past with him!" Paul grumbled. "I know how you felt about him!"

"Jings, Paul, that was twenty years ago!" Grace retorted.

"Aye, and now he's turned up, looking exactly the same and it's bound to set off some feeling of nostalgia for you. I know it would if it were me."

"Oh, would it now?" Grace asked, dropping his hand and feeling as though she had been kicked. "Well, that's good to know. Thanks for having such faith and trust in me!"

"Och, Grace, I didnae mean it like that," Paul replied, running a hand through his hair in frustration. "I overreacted. Come on, let's go back inside and enjoy the ceilidh. We need to enjoy our evening, it's Eilidh and Angus's evening, and we're here to celebrate with them."

"That's right." Grace looked at him for a long moment, as he took her hand again, and then they walked back into the ceilidh, hand in hand.

They walked back in to hear the jig winding down, to see Joe standing in the centre of the room, raising a glass of Rory's best whisky aloft as he tapped the glass.

"Ladies and gents, I'd like to raise a toast," he said, in his light, lilting voice as silence fell, and the guests took a seat, with glasses of whisky of their own, to listen.

Grace's breath caught in her throat as she caught sight of Joe's face, full of emotion as he began.

"I have to say it's been a long time since I gave a speech," Joe continued. "But I want to say a few words before tomorrow. I want you all to raise your glasses on the eve of what is gonnae be the best day of Angus and Eilidh's life. I want to say I cannae quite believe I'm not only standing here today, or that I get to watch these two lovebirds get married. My only regret is that the two people they loved cannot be here today. Annabelle, Angus's mother, and Marianne, her best friend, whom both are sorely missed especially as they loved a braw wedding... ," his voice cracked and he cleared his throat as he glanced down at his wedding ring. "I want to raise a glass to absent friends and relatives."

"To absent friends and relatives!"

Grace put an arm around Paul's waist, and smiled up at him as everyone raised a glass.

"I want to remember, on the eve of the best wedding

we're gonnae attend this year, in this beautiful Georgian mansion, uniting these two love birds. We all have been waiting for this day to come, and I think we're gonnae have a verra emotional day…"

Everyone looked over at Eilidh and Angus.

"Aye, I bet we are," Maudie beamed, wiping away a tear.

"A more wonderful couple I never did see," Joe continued, smiling across at Eilidh and Angus, eyes shining with pure happiness. "Angus and Eilidh, I can see from here how much you two adore each other, that you two have a true love that for each other. the only thing, and I speak for us all when I say this, is that we wish it happened earlier."

There was a ripple of laughter and murmurs of agreement.

"Luckily for you two, we were well aware that you two were destined for each other. But despite all that, we're overjoyed you're finally here, getting married. We cannae wait to rejoice in your love and happiness tomorrow. The same way I did on my own wedding day, to my darling Annabelle. I just wish she was here, to enjoy all this with you. Here's to Eilidh, and Angus. To a wonderful wedding!"

"To Angus and Eilidh and a wonderful wedding!" Everyone chorused, clinking their glasses together with a resounding cheer.

. . .

Rory clapped Joe on the back, and The Trinity embraced him, and Angus knew, from the misty, nostalgic look in his eyes, that he was thinking of his own wedding day, and Annabelle.

Chapter Thirteen

*T*he Past.

Winter.

In the back garden at Honeybee Cottage Marianne
Andersen stepped out onto the patio, taking care on the
icy patio, as she walked over to the beehives at the back
of the garden, and knocked on the hive.

"I've got some news, Annabelle and Joe are getting
married," she told the bees after she knocked on the
hive. It was important to tell the bees about a marriage,
birth or death. "I'll bring you a garland later."

.　.　.

"Lars?" Marianne called to her husband as she headed back inside to get ready. "We have to get to the church soon. Are you nearly ready?"

"I can't get this straight," Lars complained amiably, as he struggled with his bowtie.

"Och, come here," Marianne said, reaching out and adjusting his bowtie for him, standing on tip toe to reach him, smiling at the fact she sometimes forgot how tall and bear-like he was. Her husband, her Lars, and she smiled with love.

"There," she announced, and gave him a pat.

"Come here," Lars said and pulled her to him, kissing her passionately, and making her swoon. "You look beautiful, Mrs. Andersen."

She glanced down at her pale pink dress, and heels, her light brown hair the colour of Demerara sugar bounced attractively around her shoulders, bright blue eyes sparkling with happiness.

"Thank you. You scrub up well, Mr. Andersen."

"*Kjære.*"

Kjaere. The Norwegian word for Darling. He had taken to calling her that since their first date almost eighteen months ago. Lars's family was originally from Norway, moving over to Scotland when Lars was a toddler, and he had been brought up on the East coast. He had moved to Mossbrae to work at Cairnmhor Farm as a farmhand working for Joe, which is how he and Marianne had met.

They smiled at one another now, and he reached for his suit jacket. "Shall we go?"

Marianne took his hand in hers, loving the way it made her feel safe and protected, and nodded. As they drove to St. Anthony's, Marianne loved seeing the snow covered rolling fields, the geese flying across towards the headland, and the snowy conifer forests in the distance, her mind going back to the day they had met, eighteen months earlier.

They had met on a blind date, organised by Annabelle and Joe at The Dog and Duck, and it had been love at first sight. It had been a classic meet cute.

There was something alluring about his broad, muscular, bear like frame, sandy blond hair and dark brown eyes, and when she saw the thick set forearms beneath the rolled up sleeves of the dark navy shirt, The only word she could think of to describe him was how burly he was, like a Viking, and felt her heart race in surprise at the sight of him.

In turn, he had nearly dropped his drinks at the sight of her. She must have made a good impression though, Marianne thought now, because he had proposed six weeks later, whilst they were on their first holiday in a little cabin at the side of a loch, and they had married one warm Sunday in May at St. Anthony's church.

They parked in the car park opposite the church, walking slowly so that she didn't slip in her heels.

"I think we made it in time," Marianne whispered to Lars as they headed into the church.

It was chilly inside the church, but Marianne didn't

notice as she was enveloped by the scent of roses and white heather posies which hung at the end of every pew. She loved the little church, especially the huge stained glass window at the head of the aisle.

"Och, I couldn't think of a better place to get married! Hello, Nelly!"She greeted Nelly warmly as they joined her, Enid and Maudie at the end of their pew at the back of the church, which was full to the brim with guests. "Look how nervous Joe looks!"

She pointed over at the head of the aisle like an excited smile, dressed in his traditional family tartan looking pale with nerves, and Nelly and Maudie smiled at each other. "I'm sure he'll be fine once he sees Annabelle."

"She'll be here any moment," Maudie said, and at that moment, the Bridal March struck up, and they all turned to see Annabelle had arrived on her father's arm, dressed in a floor length gown with lace sleeves, and a garland of christmas roses in her hair.

"Och, look at Joe's face," Nelly said delighted. "All those nerves are gone."

Marianne glanced up the aisle and saw that the expression on Joe's was one of admiration and pure love for his bride-to-be.

"Ladies and gentlemen," the vicar began the vows as Annabelle reached the head of the aisle and took Joe's hands in hers with a shy smile.

Marianne felt tears well up in her eyes. "Och, I love a good wedding!"

"Aye. It's all thanks to us," Maudie said with a wink.
"That's the beauty of matchmaking for you!"

Marianne looked at Lars and smiled. "Aye, you cannae beat a good bit of matchmaking…"

"I now pronounce you husband and wife," the vicar intoned as the ceremony came to an end and the congregation erupted into noisy applause.

"Thank you, Marianne, having the reception here was a braw idea!" Annabelle cried, hugging Marianne, as Lars popped the cork on the bottle of champagne and topped up her glass. "It's so kind of you both."

"Och, it's no problem," Marianne replied, as she took a sip. "There's more than enough room for everyone."

It had been Marianne's idea to host the reception at Honeybee Cottage, a gift to their friends. After all, Annabelle had said she wanted to have somewhere cosy and quiet with it being winter, and the weather being unpredictable.

She looked around the living room now, admiring the yellow and white balloons, ribbons and banners reading JOE and ANNABELLE. Over in the dining room, Marianne had laid out a delicious buffet, of all of Joe and Annabelle's favourite foods, including, Marianne's home made honey cakes and a home made wedding cake.

. . .

Clink clink clink!

Joe stood, tapping his fork on his glass.

"I want to thank you all for being able to make the wedding today. I know the weather is hardly the one for it, but I'm glad you can all make it. I want to thank my beautiful Annabelle for marrying me and making me the happiest man alive. Ladies and gentlemen, to Mrs. Annabelle Kincaid."

Everyone raised their glasses in a toast. "To Mrs Kincaid!"

"I love you," Annabelle said, kissing him gently on the mouth.

"I love you too, Mrs. Kincaid."

They looked at each other as though they were the only ones in the room. Maudie, Nelly and Enid exchanged a knowing glance as they clinked glasses.

"Look, it's snowing!" Annabelle said and pointed out of the window. they all turned. Indeed, it was.

The snow was coming down now, covering the ground in a thin layer of snow which made it look like a postcard. It was the perfect end to the perfect day.

"It's braw," Joe said, putting his arm around her. "Good job we brought the sheep in early."

Joe glanced up at his father, Angus, and smiled at him. His father had run Cairnmhor Farm for the last thirty years and one day, he hoped to follow in his father's footsteps.

The previous week, Joe and Angus Senior had made the decision to bring the ewes down from the hillside.

The ewes usually stayed on the hillside but given the worsening weather, and the fact they were due to lamb in the following months, they had decided to bring them down to the lambing barn. Usually they used the in-byes but the weather was reported to worsen and with the possibility of early lambs, Joe and Angus Senior and knew they had made the right decision.

"Och, a good job we're celebrating today!"

"In that case, let's make the most of it," Annabelle said brightly as she turned to the CD player now and put on one of Joe's favourite jazz tracks. "How about that first dance?"

"I'd be honoured," Joe said, taking her in his arms and dancing her around the tiny living room. Everyone clapped and cheered and soon joined them, as it snowed and snowed.

Marianne joined them, and the three danced together. Lars joined them, and soon, everyone else paired up, and as the music was turned up louder, a loud voice carried across the room.

"So sorry I'm late!"

Annabelle and Marianne glanced over to see Annabelle's Uncle Cedric had arrived, lingering near the drink's cabinet. He was a tall, large man, who favoured tweeds and wellingtons no matter the occasion.

"Time for the fun part, aye? A wonderful wedding!"

This was greeted by frenzied barking as two giant Deerhounds raced past, doing zooms around the living room.

"Och, not the dogs!" Annabelle winced. "Keep them away from the buffet!"

Joe, hearing her, saved the day by heading over to Cedric, and murmuring something in his ear.

"Oh, of course, son. Huggin! Munnin! Outside!"

As the two dogs turned and charged back outside, Cedric opened the cupboard, and helped himself to the brandy.

"Och, he's started already!" Annabelle whispered urgently, and Marianne glanced over. Cedric did enjoy his brandy.

"That was a Christmas present," she murmured, glancing over with mild panic.

"Just wait until he gets on the dance floor!" Maudie teased from her left.

"Och no, Flora's here."

Annabelle's eyes widened as they glanced across at a pretty blonde woman who was about ten years older than them, dressed in a peacock blue dress with short sleeves despite the weather.

"Flora, darling! There you are!" Cedric called loudly, and poured her a brandy too. "Fancy a dance?"

Flora nodded encouragingly.

"Och, I've seen that look before," Nelly intoned, exchanging looks with Enid.

"Darling Flora, I've wanted to ask you for some time now," Cedric could be heard from the dance floor. "Would you like to have dinner with me some time?"

Flora, to everyone's chagrin, nodded.

"A better match would be more ideal," Enid intoned, as though to herself. "She isnae the right one for him..."

Marianne and Annabelle exchanged a concerned glance. Enid was one for making accurate premonitions...

"Looks a little late for that. He's smitten..." Marianne quipped.

Chapter Fourteen

resent Day.

"Huggin! Munnin! Heel, I say! Heel!"

They jumped at the sound of frenzied, excited barking and everyone turned to see two enormous Deerhounds rushing into the room.

"Och no," Grace murmured, and turned to Rory. "Protect the buffet!"

Rory took a step and blocked the dogs way to the buffet.

"Huggin! Munnin! Heel!"

Grace and Paul exchanged a glance.

"Odin's ravens..." Enid murmured solemnly. "Trouble is coming."

Maudie glanced across at the doorway, where a tall man had entered the room. Dressed in hunting tweeds and wellingtons, a tweed cap on his bald head, emphasising his round, moon face and small blue eyes.

The dogs hurried back to him at the sound of their names.

"Don't be sampling the buffet just yet!" He said with a hearty laugh, as he entered the room.

"I thought they weren't coming tomorrow?" Robyn whispered to Grace who shrugged as they watched him greet the other guests.

"There's the lovely bride to be!" Cedric announced, greeting her warmly. "I'm sorry we're late. We had to drive over from Inverness."

"Thank you," Eilidh said, politely. "It's lovely to see you again."

"Yes, I haven't seen you since Grace's wedding when you were with that ex-fiance of yours."

"Aye, I remember…" Eilidh replied.

"Good job he jilted you though, eh? Otherwise you wouldn't be here today!" He added with a hearty laugh.

"Did you have a good journey from Inverness?" Angus cut in, seeing the look on Eilidh's face.

"Ah, yes. Traffic was heavy but we're finally here. You've not met Odette yet, have you, Eilidh?"

"No, I'm looking forward to meeting her."

"Cedric! Come here man, and give your sister a hand!"

They turned to the short woman, who was dressed head to toe in black, reminding Grace of a dishevelled raven.

"Robyn!" Cedric called cheerfully. "How are you doing?"

"We're good thank you, Uncle Cedric!" She called back brightly, nudging Grace with an elbow. "Is it too late to make a run for it?"

"Far too late…" Enid intoned from her right.

"Wonderful to see you!" Cedric continued, as he ambled over and embraced her. "Right then, where are your kids? I'm surprised you haven't got a few yet! I always thought you would have a few by now.."

Robyn exchanged a look with Grace and pasted a smile on her face. "No, not yet."

"Shame. Grace has a couple now, right, Gracie?"

"Aye, we've two. Mhairi and Ollie," Grace replied, putting an arm around Robyn's shoulders as she gestured to Mhairi and Ollie who were dancing with Connie on the dance floor.

"Running a bakery now, I hear?"

"Aye, we are," Grace replied.

"They should have let you make the wedding cake!" Cedric laughed.

"They did."

"Ah, well, I bet it's wonderful." He glanced around as Joe made his way over. "Ah, there's the happy father-in-law to be. Joe, how are you? It's been years!"

"Hello, Cedric," Joe said, as he made his way over. "Good to see you."

"And you," Cedric smiled. "Shame your Annabelle isn't here too. She did love a good wedding."

"Does he know why she's not here?" Robyn whispered but Grace gave her a sharp nudge with her elbow.

"Aye," Joe said softly. "She did."

"Glad you could make it too. I heard about your heart attack. That was lucky, eh?"

"Och, I wouldnae say I was lucky, Cedric," Joe said lightly. "I had to have emergency surgery."

"Good to see you though. Shall we get a drink?"

He put an arm around Joe's shoulders, but as he walking away, he spotted The Trinity and stopped dead in his tracks.

"Enid," Cedric replied, his tone cold. "I didn't realise you three were here, but then again, I can't say I'm surprised."

"Hello, Cedric, how are you?" Enid said, turning to face him. "We're here to celebrate Eilidh and Angus, the same as you are."

"Aye. I just hope their marriage lasts a bit longer than mine did. Excuse me..."

"Cedric, wait-"

But he didn't listen, already stalking back across the room, heading for the doorway, followed by his two Deerhounds.

"Why can you no' just leave him alone!" Odette hissed. "Have you no' put him through enough?"

"Odette, we didnae put him through anything. We merely stated the fact of things…"

"You're all witches! With all your weird predictions! You shouldn't be allowed near people!" Odette carried on, as though she hadn't heard them.

"I think it's time we retired to bed," Enid

announced, and with that, she headed upstairs with Nelly and Maudie in tow.

"Should we go after them?" Robyn asked, but Grace shook her head.

"Best let everything cool down. Let's get another drink."

"Is everything alright?" Eilidh asked in alarm as she came over. "What happened with Cedric and The Trinity?"

"Enid made a prediction a few years ago at my wedding," Grace explained. "She predicted that Flora, Cedric's wife, and he weren't suited, and that she would leave him for the true love of her life, and she did, six months later, but what's worse, is that their daughter, Meg, cut contact with Cedric after. Cedric and Odette blamed her, saying she had given Flora and Meg ideas."

"Och, that's so sad," Eilidh replied. "I actually feel sorry for him, despite him accidentally insulting everyone. What can we do to make things right?"

"There's verra little we can do right now," Grace sighed. "It's getting late, and if we're gonnae be fit for purpose tomorrow, we should head to bed."

"A grand idea," Eilidh and Robyn agreed. "But there's no' gonnae be any trouble is there?"

Grace shook her head. "No, there's no' any trouble, dinnae fret yourself…"

"In that case, goodnight. See you both in the morning."

"Aye, I'd better get the kids to bed," Grace added, glanced across at the who were curled up in a faded armchair each, snoring softly, and had luckily missed all the drama.

"I think," Angus said, his words slightly slurred as he checked his watch. "We should go to bed…Big day tomorrow…"

"Come on," Orion grinned, putting his arm around Angus's shoulders. "Paul and I will help get you to bed. Now, no sneaking into the bridal suite in the middle of the night, you can bunk with me."

"Aye, dinnae want to spoil the surprise," Angus agreed with a nod, as Orion and Paul helped him out of the room.

"At least he's had a good night…" Grace smiled.

"Aye, he's no' the only one either," Robyn agreed. "Since Angus is in our room tonight, I might bunk in with you, and I'll give you a hand with the kids."

"Thanks, at least we willnae have problems getting them to sleep."

They said goodnight to everyone and headed out of the room, carrying the kids out.

"Hey, I've just realised, it'll be like when we were kids! Have you a torch? We can exchange messages!" Robyn said, as they entered Grace and Paul's room, which was a smaller version of the bridal suite. It was light and airy, and the warm night breeze gently drifted in the open bay window.

"Och! I remember you used to do that every Christmas! Ma used to glance under the door to make sure we were asleep."

"I remember!" Robyn said softly, her eyes misting over. "I wish she was here."

"Me too," Grace said, pulling her close. "She'd have been so proud."

Robyn nodded silently as she helped put the kids to bed.

"Apart from that exchange with The Trinity, it's been a lovely night. Especially Da's speech…"

"Aye, it was so lovely to see him. I cannae believe he's here and able to do a speech tomorrow."

"I know," Robyn agreed. "He's doing well now isn't he. I cannae believe we nearly lost him. And he misses Ma so much."

Grace took her hand, and squeezed it. "I miss her too."

"Every day…"

They fell silent, lost in thought.

"Would you ever want another baby?" Robyn asked, breaking the silence.

Grace shook her head, a little sadly, Robyn noticed. "I think we're too late to start all over again, and I dinnae think I have the energy. Why?"

"Och, no reason…" Robyn murmured. "You know Orion and I are trying for a baby?"

"Aye. How is it going?" Grace sat up and reaching

for her hand. "I'm sorry about Cedric's comment."

Robyn shrugged. "We've no news yet…Orion keeps telling me to take it one day at a time… I'm trying not to let it get me down…"

"Aye,"Dinnae fret, Orion's right," Grace assured her. "Dinnae let it fret you too much. Let's enjoy the wedding, take your mind off the worry."

"You know, and I bet it sounds silly, but I'd love to be the type of mum you are when it happens."

Grace glanced at her in surprise. "What do you mean?"

"I see you with Mhairi and Ollie and you remind me so much of Ma, and how she was when we were wee. You're so patient, and kind, and gentle. Like a Super Mum," Robyn replied. "I'm sorry for all the horrible things I said at the hen do."

"No, I needed to hear them, and I needed a wake up call. Robyn, I'm no' a super mum. I find it so hard to parent sometimes, I'm grateful for the bakery to keep me on an even keel!" Grace gave a wry laugh. "I'm permanently exhausted, and I hardly get to see Paul, it's tiring."

"We're all trying our best," Robyn replied, resting her head back on the pillows.. "But think of it this way, it could be worse."

"In what way?"

"You could have ended up married to that horrible Archie."

"Och, Jings! That would be an absolute nightmare!" Grace cried as they both started to laugh.

Chapter Fifteen

he Past.

Winter.

Cairnmhor Farm.

"Och! Would you look at the sky. Any moment now, you can fair see the flakes starting to fall…" Joe commented to Annabelle as he carried the champagne to the dining room.

"Aye, I'm glad you brought the ewes down and put them in the lambing shed early," Annabelle agreed. At the best of times, sheep were unpredictable, and Joe didn't want any early lambers out in this weather. Winters could be particularly harsh here in the Inner Hebrides, with blizzards and gale force winds bringing everything to a halt, and access to Mossbrae grinding to a halt if the ferries were cancelled. "And everyone made it in time despite the weather!"

There were shrieks and a round of applause as Joe popped the cork, and poured everyone a glass.

"Happy anniversary!" Joe announced as he poured Annabelle a glass.

"Happy anniversary," Annabelle grinned. "I cannae believe it's been twenty years already!"

Maudie sipped her champagne and nodded. "Och, we knew you two were gonnae be for the long haul."

Joe put an arm around Annabelle's waist and kissed her passionately on the mouth to whoops and cheers from the rest of the party. "I love you, Mrs Kincaid."

Annabelle kissed him back with a grin. "I love you, Mr. Kincaid."

She took a sip of her champagne. "Och, we need to get some food."

"Aye," Joe replied. "We've Gracie to thank for that!"

They went through to the dining room where Grace had prepared a delicious buffet.

"All your favourites!" Grace announced brightly.

"Och, that's braw!" Annabelle enthused. "You're gonnae do really well on this catering course."

"We've only been there a term," Grace replied, turning to her mum and giving her a hug. "We're just learning the basics, and next term, we're learning how to make pastry next term."

"And what time is the wonderful Archie arriving?" Maudie asked.

"Any minute now, he's in a taxi," Grace replied, checking her watch, unable to keep the grin off her face.

"The look of love if ever we saw one," Maudie swooned in her pale pink jumper which matched her candy floss pink hair.

"Gracie wants to marry him!" Robyn teased as she passed them, making kissing noises.

"Och, behave yourself and grab some food!" Grace cried, giving her a playful swat.

Robyn, grinning headed to the buffet table and piled her plate high. Grace always thought it should have been Robyn who should have been a chef, as she loved food so much. Robyn lived to eat, not eat to live, and she had always been that way. Whilst Grace loved her for it, she thought Robyn was a bit of gannet sometimes.

"What's all this?" Joe asked, making his way over to them as he got some food for The Trinity, who were on the sofa, catching up with Eilidh and Marianne. Over the opposite side of the room, Angus was chatting to Jim Sinclair, who was visiting Mossbrae for the Christmas period. "Are we talking about your young man again, Gracie?"

"Och, just planning the wedding!" Annabelle teased.

"We've only been seeing each other a month," she protested. "We've only just moved on from being friends…"

"Och, that's a good foundation for a strong rela-tionship."

"Aye, that's true," Nelly added enthusiastically. "I was friends with my darling Albert when we first met."

"Aye, I agree," said Annabelle, turning to Joe. "We were friends when we first got together didn't we?"

"Och, well, I remember I proposed to you before we had our first date," Joe replied, with a grin.

"Aye, you did. But we were friends too."

"I think I can hear the doorbell!" She called, heading through the dining room towards the front door where the dogs were barking with frantic excitement.

"Hello! Come in, welcome to Cairnmhor," Grace said shyly as she opened the door to him. "Dinnae mind the dogs, they willnae hurt you."

"Hello," Archie said as she gently moved the dogs aside, and he bent to kiss her. "It's good to see you. So this is your home."

"Aye, it is," Grace said proudly, gesturing to the kitchen, and he looked around impassively. "Come on through, everyone is keen to meet you."

"Right," Archie replied, keeping his shoes on as he followed her through to the living room.

"Everyone! This is Archie!" Grace said proudly.

"Och, he's handsome!" Maudie whispered, and Nelly nodded.

"Pleased to meet you, Archie," Annabelle stepped forward and shook his hand. "I'm Grace's mother, Annabelle."

"Pleased to meet you," Archie replied, taking them all in, impassively.

"When's the wedding?" Robyn called over mischievously.

"Ignore my sister," Grace whispered. "Shall we get you a drink? Some food? I made it all myself. Oh, Da, this is Archie."

She turned to Joe, who regarded Archie coolly.

"Hello," Joe said, extending his hand to shake Archie's, who shook it back, coolly. "I'm Joe. I've heard all there is to know about you. So you're Grace's boyfriend, aye?"

"I suppose you could say that, yes," Archie said, with a smile at Grace who was looking adoringly at him.

"Come on, son, get a plate," Annabelle encouraged, and Grace gave him a little shove towards the table.

"Is he a city boy?" Enid asked, glancing over at him, and Grace nodded.

"He's got very smooth hands," Enid replied. "All the chefs I've known have rough hands."

"He's in training," Grace protested.

"Take care with this one, for he is not as he seems…"

Grace frowned at her lightly. "But we are happy, Enid."

"Aye, but remember," Enid warned. "Do not lose your friends in the pursuit of love."

Grace nodded solemnly but she loved Enid like a grandmother, and trusted her.

"Come and get food," Enid replied, putting an arm around her.

. . .

148

Archie came back with some food and sat down in the corner. Immediately the dogs were around him, sniffing curiously.

"They'll no' bite you, son. they're more interested in the food," he said, as he called the dogs to him, seeing Archie flinch away, regarding the dogs with disdain. "Well, maybe the pup but she's teething."

"Alright," Archie said coolly, sitting rigidly in his chair.

Joe noticed the way he looked around the kitchen with disdain as though he was too good to be standing here. As though he was too good for them.

"He willnae be around long," Enid intoned, as she passed him. "She will meet the one for her soon enough."

"Aye, let's hope so."

"Hi Archie, I'm Angus, Grace's brother," Angus said, taking a seat next to him, and keen to start a conversation. "Do you know anything about farming?"

Archie shook his head.

"I'm not that bothered about farming to be honest. Grace was telling me how much she's not keen on staying in farming. Especially lambing."

"I said it makes me feel sick, the smell. I didnae say I didnae like it," Grace protested.

Suddenly, Archie's phone blared into life, and putting down his plate, she went to answer it.

"Excuse me."

The conversation drifted to more idle chatter, and before she realised, almost twenty minutes had passed, and frowning, she put her plate to one side.

"Where's Archie? He's been on the phone a while."

"He's been gone a long time," Joe murmured about ten minutes later when Archie hadn't returned to the table. The height of bad manners in their home.

"No' gone, is he?" Joe joked as he took a slurp of tea. "Look out the kitchen window."

"Whisht, Da. He'll hear you," Grace chided him gently. "I'll go and check on him…"

"You'll sit there and finish your food," Annabelle cut in. "You'll no' be chasing after him."

"Och, I'm no' doing that," Grace laughed. "I dinnae want him to be making a bad impression."

"Och, I think he can manage that on his own. City boy, is he?"

"Aye, he is, actually," Grace replied.

"I could tell by his hand shake. He's got the softest hands I've ever shaken."

"Och, Da," Grace murmured. "You cannae judge folk on a handshake."

"No?" Joe murmured. "It tells you a lot about a person."

He finished his meal. "I'll go and round him up. Shall I take wee Betty with me? She needs the practice."

"Da!"

Joe smiled back at her and headed out to the porch, ready to call him back to the table when the conversation made him pause.

"Yeah, I'm over at Mossbrae this weekend," Archie was saying, standing with his back to him. Joe watched him for a moment, just so that he wouldn't think he was deliberately listening in. He didn't care who he was chatting to, but Archie seemed to have forgotten that he was visiting his girlfriend's parents the first time, and that it was important to make a good impression. But maybe that was just him being old fashioned. He wasn't sure. That was until he heard the rest of the conversation…

Joe felt his fist clench at the sound of those poisonous words. How dare he, the cheeky little shit. He wondered what Grace would say if he punched him on the nose and sent him packing.

"No," Archie gave a soft chuckle. "I'd rather be back in London, not out here in the sticks…I'm at Grace's parents. They own a farm. Exactly, it's the usual shit hole. Stinks of animals. Makes me want to vomit."

Joe couldn't bear to hear any more. Clearing his throat, he opened the porch door, hit with a blast of cold air, and closed the door behind him.

"I've got to go," Archie murmured and ended the call.

"If it wasnae gonnae upset Grace further," Joe cut in, "I'd ask you to go right now, you cheeky little shit."

"Excuse me?"

"It's a shit hole here, eh? You're at your girlfriend's parent's home. It's spotlessly clean, and if it does smell of animals, it's because you're on a farm. I know it isnae for everyone, but you dinnae seem to have any manners.

You're rude, impolite, and what's more, you're Ana entitled wee shite."

Archie raised an eyebrow.

"I'd ask you to leave, but I care about Grace. She's my daughter and I love her," Joe snorted. "I heard the rest. You're cheating on Grace."

"I care about Grace too."

"If you did, you'd show more respect and make an effort," Joe said, going into protective dad mode, and rolling up his sleeves. "Now, you get your skinny little arse back in that dining room. This is my wedding anniversary and I'll no' have trouble in my house. Grace has invited you, but I can ask you to leave. I like decent, honest, people, and you, are neither. You're spoiling my wedding anniversary, so I hope after tonight, I never see your face again. Until then, you will behave yourself in my house. Do you understand?"

Archie paled. "I understand."

Joe pushed the door open and headed back to the dining room, followed by a shame face Archie, who sat for the rest of the party, shell shocked.

There was a crack of glass, and everyone turned to see Enid's wine glass lay broken on the floor.

"Trouble is brewing…" Enid murmured as Grace leapt forward to clean it up. "We need all treasure this evening."

"Treasure it?" Grace murmured, feeling anxiety gnaw in the bit of her stomach as she glanced at Archie who was busy texting on his phone and didn't meet her eye.

"Excuse me, I need some air,." Annabelle said, and headed outside for some fresh air.

Marianne passed Annabelle as she headed outside to the back garden.

"Are you alright, hen?"

"What? Aye, I'm alright, just feeling a bit hot," Annabelle replied, with a wry smile.

"Are you sure? You look pale."

Annabelle pushed the door open and headed outside, as an icy blast of air hit her in the face, and she sighed with relief.

"Ah, that's better. I've been feeling dizzy."

Marianne took a step forward. "How long have you been having dizzy spells?"

"A little while, but it's the pain in my side."

"Annabelle, you need to get it checked out," Marianne murmured, taking her hand. "Shall I tell Joe? I can go and get him…"

"Och, no, dinnae fret him. It's our anniversary. I dinnae want him to worry."

Marianne put an arm around her. "How often are you getting these pains?"

"A few weeks now," Annabelle replied. "It started in the shower. I thought it was something I'd eaten but then it went away."

"It's no' appendicitis?" Marianne asked, but Annabelle shook her head. "I havenae got an appendix. It had it removed as a child, so it isnae that."

"Then the first thing you need to do is go and see a doctor. I can come with you."

"Aye, I will," Annabelle assured her. "I'll call them first thing in the morning."

"Hen, I'm here for you," Marianne said, pulling her into a hug. "No matter what happens."

"Thanks, Marianne," Annabelle replied. "I know I can rely on you."

Chapter Sixteen

 resent Day.

The following morning, Grace woke early on the morning of the wedding, admiring the beautiful views as she pulled on a light green blouse and jeans to head downstairs to assemble the cake before the ceremony, her heart racing with excited happiness. She couldn't wait to see Eilidh and Angus's faces when they saw the cake…

It was beautifully cool in the kitchen, as Grace felt the hot sun through the open windows as she walked towards cupboards where she and Rhona had left the cakes.

"Morning! Oh, Leanna, it's you! How lovely to see

you!" Grace cried and gave the young blonde woman a hug.

"Hello! Aye, that's right! You're Grace! Gran's just dealing with the starters for later on. She'll be back in a moment. It's a gorgeous morning for a wedding, aye?" Leanna said cheerfully.

"It is. It's been years. How are you? Rhona said you're training to be a baker too."

"That's right," Leanna replied, beaming. "I'm hoping to open my own bakery, like you, one day."

"That's wonderful!" Grace replied. "Rhona was telling me yesterday, she's so proud."

"Aye, she is. I want to move to Edinburgh, as I love the city, but I dinnae like to leave Gran. She gets so lonely now that she's single again."

"Aye," Grace nodded in agreement.

"She willnae admit it, but she gets lonely." said Leanna conspiratorially. "I was hoping there's someone here at the wedding I could set her up with…"

"Is that so?"

Grace looked at her as though seeing her for the first time, and then, she thought about Cedric and The Trinity, and had an idea.

"I might be able to help you out there…" she replied, with a smile. "But first, I need to get this cake assembled before the wedding!"

"Ooh, I've heard all about the cake. I cannae wait to see it," Leanna gushed, adding with a shy smile. "I've been inspired by you. I follow you on Insta. I love the cakes you bake!"

"I'll let you have a sneak peek!" Grace replied as she got the stool and opened the cupboard. "I've put them in here..."

She reached inside the cupboard but there were no boxes...

"Och!" Grace cried, patting the shelf frantically, and finding nothing. "They were in here... Rhona and I put them on this shelf. I cannae see it!" She looked in the back of the cupboard but she couldn't see it.

"Is everything alright?" Rhona asked as she entered the kitchen.

"I cannae find the cake!" Grace cried, turning to her in panic. "Could it have been moved?"

"I havenae checked the cupboard since last night hen, but it could have been moved by one of the catering team."

Grace gave a groan of despair and started looking in the neighbouring cupboards but only found pots, pans and utensils.

"No luck," she said, shaking her head. "Och, the ceremony's in five hours!"

"Dinnae fret hen, it's still early, we have time to find the cake," Rhona assured her. "Leanna and I will keep looking."

"But what can we do if we dinnae find the cake? Och, I want to cry," Grace's voice cracked with emotion. "I wanted it to be perfect for Eilidh and Angus and now it's ruined!"

〜

In the bridal suite, Eilidh looked out of the bay window, lost in thought, her mind reeling with something more important than her nerves about the wedding.

Her period was late.

Only a few days, but she was beginning to wonder, especially after the conversation she and Angus had had, and was glad that she had brought an early response pregnancy test with her.

Climbing off the chaise longe, she headed to the suitcase, where the test was hidden in an inside pocket where Angus wouldn't look and find it before she had time to tell him.

But when she reached in the pocket, there was no test and she started.

"Where is it?" She murmured, frowning, and for a moment, she retraced her steps in her head, surmising it must be somewhere along the corridor, and clapped a hand over her mouth. What if someone found it and jumped to the wrong conclusion?

There was a soft knock on the door, and she stood up, heading for the doorway.

"Hello, hen!" Connie said, opening her arms and enveloping her in a warm hug. She was wearing a lavender blue suit, her shoulder length brown hair and blue eyes so like Marianne now. "Did you sleep well?"

"Aye," Eilidh replied, with a nod.

"Grace and Robyn are heading downstairs for breakfast. Shall I ask Rhona to bring you up some breakfast?" Connie continued, as she entered the room, and gasped aloud at Eilidh's dress, hanging on the en-suite door frame. "Look at the embroidery, it's so beautiful. Marianne would be so proud."

Her voice cracked with emotion, and Eilidh put an arm around her shoulders.

"I wish she was here," Eilidh murmured.

"She is always with you," Connie replied, turning and stroking her cheek. "She would be so happy to see you and Angus wed. Dinnae be nervous. Everything will go smoothly."

"Unlike last time…"

"Och, it's normal to think of the past when we're making a life changing decision," Connie said softly. "But dinnae fret, Angus is the right one for you. You're making the right choice."

"I know I am," Eilidh replied confidently. "It's just nerves, the thought of standing up in front of everyone."

"Angus has to do the same," Connie reminded her gently. "You're in it together."

"Aye, we are," Eilidh replied, thinking about him now, and felt at that moment, all her worries fade.

"We might still find it yet," Leanna told Grace reassuringly. "It's probably been moved in time for the cake cutting."

"But I havenae had chance to assemble it yet. Do you think the catering team are doing it instead? Eilidh has put me in charge of the cake though…"

"I think the best thing to do," Rhona suggested. "Is for you to go and find Archie."

"I need to make another cake."

"We can do that," Leanna cut in. "If you find the original cake, we'll have a spare one, so it willnae be a problem."

Grace shook her head. "It should be me. I cannae expect you to do it all."

"Hen, look, we're here to help you, so let us help," Rhona said gently. "Now, go and find Archie, and then you can go and get changed for the wedding. Leanna and I will keep you updated."

"Alright," Grace relented. "Thank you so much, you're so kind."

"That's what friends are for," Rhona replied, patting her shoulder and Leanna assured her with a nod. "Now, what kind of cake did Eilidh and Angus want?"

Grace outlined the details of the cake, as Leanna wrote them down.

"Where could I find Archie?" Grace asked when Leanna was done.

"He'll have just arrived," Rhona said, checking her watch. "You might be able to catch him by the front entrance before he starts for the day."

"Thank you," Grace said. "I'll speak to him and get back to you as quick as I can."

"Hen," Rhona added as she turned to leave. "Dinnae fret, alright? Everything is gonnae turn out alright."

Grace felt tears spring to her eyes as she was overwhelmed with relief. "Thank you both, so much."

. . .

She headed along the corridors towards the front entrance, looking out for any sign of Archie when there was a creak of footsteps on the stairs, and she turned.

"Ma! Can we have pancakes for breakfast, please?" Mhairi called as she clutched Robyn's hand.

"I couldnae keep them upstairs for a second longer, sorry," Robyn replied as she led them downstairs.

"Where's Da?" Ollie asked, as he took Grace's hand.

"Here I am, everything alright?" Paul called softly from the landing. "Is anyone else awake?"

They jumped at the sound of clinks of tea cups and laughter coming from the dining room.

"I think that answers the question," Grace quipped as Paul reached her.

"What's wrong? Last minute nerves about the cake?"

"Aye, something like that," she replied, as he took her hand.

"Come on, you look like you need a brew."

Grace glanced back, hesitating and then at the sound of her stomach rumbling, she followed them into the dining room.

The dining room was impressive, light and airy, painted heritage blue, with a vast Georgian fireplace in the centre of one wall, and long oak dining table opposite.

"Ah, there they are! We wondered where you were!" Maudie called brightly. "Come and have some breakfast."

"There's plenty of everything," Rory said brightly, looking particularly bright eyed given the amount of whisky he had drunk last night..

"This looks lovely!" Grace said. glancing at the plates of bacon, sausage, potato scones, hash browns and black pudding, and buttermilk pancakes. There were also mushrooms, white pudding, tomatoes and scrambled eggs, as well as jugs of orange juice and water, a pot of coffee and a tea pot laid out. "There's even smoked kippers!"

"I think they're calling my name," Paul grinned, helping himself to a couple. "Those potato scones look great too, eh, Gracie?"

"Looks like you're not the only one who's fond of potato scones," Maudie clucked, glancing over at William who was chomping away heartily on one from his highchair.

"He's got a braw appetite," Grace agreed with a warm smile as she helped herself.

"We'll have to get the recipe for your potato scones," Isla said. Even she looked like she had just returned home from a holiday abroad as opposed to a broken night with a baby, her red hair fastened into a neat plait down her back, complimenting her pale pink T-shirt and jeans, as William finished his potato scone and reached for another from his mother's plate. "He loves them."

"Me too!" Mhairi announced. "Can I have some more sausages?"

"Aye, of course you can!" Rory replied, piling up her plate. "You need all your energy today being a bridesmaid. It's a busy job."

"Is it really?" Mhairi asked.

"Aye, besides Eilidh and Angus, you two have the most important jobs," Rory said solemnly.

Ollie and Mhairi cheered.

Grace discreetly checked her watch. It was almost eight now, and time was running out for her to speak to Archie about the cake, and wondering if Rhona and Leanna could pull off making and decorating another one in case she failed to find the first one. What had happened to it? she wondered, telling herself that it was merely a case the catering team had moved it, and that it wasn't actually missing...

She really hoped, given all the time and effort she had put into the cake, and that this was the case, and that they would find it.

She really didn't want to ruin Angus and Eilidh's day...

"Is everything alright?" Paul murmured to her, and Grace looked at him in surprise as he added mischievously. "You dinnae have a hangover, do you? I know I do..."

"No, it's not a hangover," Grace replied, shaking her head. "I think it's just nerves about today."

"Can I tempt you to some bacon and eggs? Potato scone?"

"Go on, then," she relented, watching as Robyn fell on her breakfast as though she'd hardly eaten that week, devouring everything within minutes, and raised an eyebrow. "The Highland air making you hungry, Robyn?"

"Something like that," Robyn replied. "Can you pass the kippers, Rory? I'm famished!"

"Aye, of course," Rory said, passing them over.

"I didnae know you liked kippers, I thought you didnae like the smell..." Orion murmured, and Robyn shrugged.

"Och! I've seen everything now," Joe grinned as he got his own breakfast. "Robyn eating kippers? Annabelle used to make kippers every weekend. She used to dip them in flour and fry them. It made the whole house smell like a smoker for hours afterwards, but I didnae mind. You cannae beat a kipper for breakfast. Although, your Ma only really loved them when she was..."

He trailed off as Maudie finished her breakfast, dabbing her chin delicately with a napkin and exchanged a glance with Enid and Nelly.

Grace glanced at Robyn now, and then back at Joe. If Robyn had news, she was certain she would tell everyone in her own time. Especially after all her tragedy before. She didn't want to dwell on that, knowing how unhappy and grief stricken her little sister had been. But it would be wonderful news if she was pregnant, and able to hold a baby in her arms this time round. Ma had revealed one time that she had lost a baby between Angus and Robyn, and Grace remembered now how much it had broken her heart. She had longed for a baby and soon, Robyn had come along. They called them rainbow babies nowadays. Grace hoped Robyn would have her own rainbow soon enough...

"A surprise revelation is on the horizon," Enid said stoically as she ate her own breakfast.

Robyn coughed loudly as she finished her kippers. "We'd better go and see if the bride is ready yet," Robyn added, and scraped back her chair. "Excuse me, I'm gonnae go and get changed."

"I'll follow you out," Grace replied, scraping back her own chair. "We need to get the kids ready."

"Not long until show time," Joe added, and as everyone else finished breakfast, and left the room. "Time to go and get ready. We've a wedding to prepare for!"

Chapter Seventeen

*G*race made her way out of the dining room and looked up the hall to the main entrance to see if she could see Archie before they had to go upstairs and get ready.

"Are you coming?" Paul asked as they reached the stairs.

"I just need to check something about the cake. I'll see you upstairs in a few minutes," Grace replied, her mind focused on the cake. "Can you help the kids get ready?"

"I want Mummy to help me," Mhairi replied, but Paul took her hand.

"I'll be up in a few moments. Promise," Grace said quickly.

"Come on," Paul said, taking the kid's hands and ushered them upstairs.

Grace watched them go, and then hurried out to find Archie, and find out where the cake was.

. . .

She strode out onto the front drive, shielding her eyes from the early morning sunlight, as she looked down the driveway, admiring the gorgeous views of the rolling countryside, conifer trees in the distance. Then, she felt a jolt of relief to see Archie loading boxes into the boot of his Range Rover.

"Archie!" She called, her shoes crunching across the gravel towards him. "I've been looking for you."

"Oh, really?" He asked as he closed the boot door closed with a bang. This morning, he was wearing jeans and a green polo shirt, and she realised he looked exactly the same as he had twenty years ago. He had the same lean, tall frame, dark hair, and when he turned to her, his piercing blue eyes and sharp cheekbones, giving him a hawkish appearance. "Is everything alright?"

"No, not really," she replied, feeling a little award. The heat of the day already spreading across the front lawn, and she felt sweat beading at her temples. "I've gone to assemble the cake and I cannae find it. Have you seen the boxes anywhere? You were there with Rhona last night when I put the boxes in the cupboard in the kitchen."

"No, I'm sorry, I haven't seen them," Archie replied, shaking his head. "I've not been down to the kitchens yet, but I'll go and speak to the team, see if they've found them."

"Thank you," Grace replied, feeling a surge of relief.

"I'm sure they will turn up though," Archie replied, placing a reassuring hand on her arm. "There's time to find them before the cake cutting."

"Thanks," Grace said with a sigh of relief, and took a step back as there was an awkward pause between them.

"I didn't get chance to congratulate you on the Visit Scotland article," he added. "You've done really well for yourself."

"Thank you."

His mobile sprang into life, breaking the tension between them, and he glanced at it.

"Sorry, I have to go. What's your plan whilst we try and find the cake?"

"Rhona and Leanna are gonnae make another one, so at least we'll have a spare cake if the original one appears. I'm hoping it does."

"Try not to fret," Archie replied. "I have to take this call now, sorry. It's one of my suppliers."

Grace nodded, and turned, heading back into the house. As she did, a blackbird gave a shrill alarm call, and glancing up, she saw Paul watching them in their bedroom window. He held her gaze for a moment, then moved away, and with a sigh, Grace headed back into the house.

As she hurried upstairs, she passed the paintings on the stairs, but as she reached the top of the stairs, she frowned in alarm.

The Landseer painting was missing.

Robyn hurried along the corridor towards her and Orion's bedroom, her mind dwelling on the conversation at breakfast when she tripped on the carpet.

"*Och! Jings!*"

Glancing down, she saw something blue and frowned. It couldn't be…

Glancing around to make sure there was no-one else around, picked up the pregnancy test. It was still in the wrapper so it was new, but her mind raced. Whose was it? Grace? Eilidh? Maybe even Isla? Another wedding guest?

Picking it up, and thinking of what Enid had said on the bus, she felt it had been more than pure coincidence that she found it…

"Ma!" Mhairi called as she pushed open their bedroom door to find Mhairi struggling as Paul tried in vain to calm her down.

"I dinnae want to wear my cardigan! I'm too warm! Ollie doesnae have to wear one!"

"Just listen to Daddy!" Ollie shouted back.

"Ollie! Whist! Mhairi, you need to listen to your Da. Wear the cardigan for the ceremony and the photos and then take it off," Grace said firmly, and relenting, Mhairi obediently put it on.

"Good," Grace replied. "Now, I'm gonnae get ready. We need to get to the bridal suite."

"Aye, but you've time to stand chatting to your ex-boyfriend," Paul muttered.

"What?" Grace asked as she pulled on the sage green floral dress.

"You heard me," Paul muttered as he fastened her zip for her. "You two looked quite cosy."

"Och, Paul, you've got it wrong," Grace cried.

"Aye?" Paul replied, coldly, and she turned to face him.

"You said he was the last person you wanted to see, and then, I see you together, and you're thick as thieves."

"He's in charge of the catering team today," Grace explained but he gave a shrug. "I was discussing the cake with him."

"If you say so," he replied, and Grace knew she needed to tell him the truth.

"Paul. I need to tell you something important. You've got the wrong end of the stick."

Paul let out an exasperated sigh." Gracie we're running late. We dinnae have time to talk about it now."

"I know, but you need to listen."

Paul put a hand on her arm. "Go and find Robyn. We have a wedding to attend."

"Fine, we'll talk about it later."

Sighing, Grace gathered the kids, and headed out to Robyn and Orion's room.

Discreetly, Robyn went into their bedroom and closed the door behind her, heart hammering. If she took the test, she would know in three minutes.

But could she do it?

She lifted her T-shirt, glancing at the small scar across her lower stomach, the only reminder she had of the baby they had lost, and felt grief hit her, like a punch in the stomach as she remembered that day, the day she had found out she was pregnant. Her periods were irregular, so not knowing when she was actually due on, she had taken a test, not expecting anything to come of it, and had been knocked sideways at the sight of two lines, and they had both burst into tears at the prospect of becoming parents.

But, heartbreakingly, it wasn't meant to be...

Her breath came out as a ragged sob as she tried not to burst into tears thinking of the day of their twelve week scan.

She had collapsed on the morning of her scan, thinking it was blood pressure, and she thanked god that Orion had been there, and being able to immediately take her to hospital where she had learnt her pregnancy was ectopic, and she had had to have an emergency tubal ligature surgery, to save her life.

A month later, she had had a follow up appointment.

"Will we ever be able to have a baby?" She remembered asking the doctor.

"Due to your pregnancy being ectopic, and as a result of your surgery to remove your fallopian tube," the doctor had gently explained, "the chances of you having another baby are reduced, but it's not impossible. You can certainly get pregnant again, if you wish to, but it may take a little longer."

"Is it likely we'll have another ectopic pregnancy?" The doctor shook his head. "No, I would say not."

Robyn had breathed a sigh of relief. So what if it took a little bit longer, she thought, it could and would happen again.

She always had hope.

That had been nearly three years ago, and she and Orion had been trying for six months, and she daren't dare to hope it would happen again.

Glancing down at the test in her hand she let out a ragged sigh. This was her chance, like someone somewhere was showing her a sign.

Hands shaking, she unwrapped the test, and decided to bite the bullet. "I can do this," she told herself, and headed into the ensuite, where she took the test and set her mobile for three minutes.

Heading back into the bedroom, she got changed for the wedding, trying to distract herself, by changing into her wedding outfit: a purple floral shift dress with matching heels and was styling her hair.

The alarm made her jump, smudging her mascara, and she hurried into the ensuite.

She looked down at the test, and felt a lump in her throat.

"Och, Jings! It cannae be true…"

Her mind swooped with a jangled mix of joy, fear and excitement, and she burst into tears, stifling her sobs as she read the words she had wanted to read for so long.

PREGNANT

2-3 weeks

"Robyn! Are you nearly ready? We need to get going to see to Eilidh!"

The urgent knocking on the door made her jump again, and Robyn hastily grabbed a tissue, blew her nose, and slipped the test into her clutch bag.

"Coming!" Robyn called, hiding the test in her bag, hurrying to the door.

She didn't want to suddenly hit Grace with her news, not right now, not when it was Eilidh's day.

"Are you alright?" Grace asked, her brow creasing lightly as she saw her face.

"Aye, I'm fine," Robyn said, brightly. "What about you? Are you alright? You were miles away at breakfast. What's going on?"

"I'm fine," Grace said, not meeting her sister's eye.

"Gracie, dinnae give me that," Robyn snorted. "This is me you're speaking to. Have you and Paul fallen out? You've no' had a stramash, aye?"

"No! Everything is fine between Paul and I. I'm just so tired. I'm blaming it on the Highland air."

She emphasised her point by stifling a yawn.

"Me too!" Robyn cried. "I slept for eight hours and I'm still shattered!"

"We're not used to it," Grace grinned, throwing her arm around her shoulders, feeling happy she had thrown Robyn off the scent.

"So have you had chance to check the cake?" Robyn asked, making her pause as they reached the bridal suite. "I bet it looks braw, aye? Wait... something's happened."

"What? No. I've checked the cake and it's braw."

"Gracie, I can tell when you're lying," Robyn said, taking her to one side. "What's going on?"

Grace met her eye, and knew she couldn't lie to Robyn. Her little sister had a sixth sense when it came to mistruths.

"The cake is missing."

"Jings, Gracie, what are you gonnae do?" Robyn asked, her eyes widening in panic. "Where did you lose the cake?"

"I went to assemble it this morning but it's gone. Rhona said she's gonnae help me look for it whilst we're helping Eilidh. She also suggested talking to the head of the catering team."

"Have you spoken to them?"

"Him. Aye, I have, and you'll never guess who it is."

"Who?" Robyn asked, agog.

"Archie Lennox."

"Your ex-boyfriend. Are you joking? What the hell is he doing here? Did you get to talk to him?"

"Rory asked him to do the catering for the day. But I

174

asked him and he doesnae know where it is, but he said he'd speak to the team."

"And you believe him, do you?" Robyn asked incredulously.

"I have to."

"What are you going to do in the meantime?" Robyn asked anxiously.

"Rhona and Leanna are gonnae make another cake, so if the first one appears we have a spare cake."

"Have you got time?"

"Aye, we have. We need to. How can we face Eilidh and Angus without a cake though? I dinnae want to let Eilidh down. It's their big day and all I want is it to be perfect. For her, and for Angus."

"You are so kind hearted," Robyn replied, putting an arm around her. "I bet Eilidh and Angus dinnae give a care about the cake. They are probably more than happy to have you here to celebrate with them."

"Robyn, they will care about the cake though. I put a lot of time and effort into that cake…We cannae let Eilidh down, especially after what happened before. It's bound to be playing on her mind today."

Robyn nodded in agreement. "You're right. We need to make sure they have a perfect day. Look, we'd better go and help her get ready."

"Robyn, wait," she cried, taking Robyn by her shoulders. "Listen to me. There are other things missing too, the Landseer painting is missing."

Her sister's eyes widened. "And no-one else has noticed?"

"I dinnae know. But you need to promise me something," Grace said desperately. "We need to keep quiet about this whilst I try and get tot the bottom of what's going on. But we cannae tell anyone, not even Orion. And especially not Eilidh, or Angus!"

Chapter Eighteen

*I*n Orion and Robyn's room, Angus was oblivious to all the goings on as he finished his delicious full Scottish breakfast, when Joe knocked on the door, and entered the room.

"Looking braw, Da," Angus said as he greeted Joe, admiring his matching kilt and navy suit jacket. "I'm wondering if I can get my jacket fastened after that breakfast!"

All the groomsmen were wearing traditional dress today of dark navy suit jacket, white shirt and formal Kincaid tartan kilt, a lovely mix of emerald green and navy.

"Aye, breakfast was braw. You cannae beat a good kipper for breakfast."

Joe took a seat, and Angus glanced over at his father now, admiring how healthy he looked today. It was almost difficult to believe, Angus thought, that last year, Joe had had heart surgery following a cardiac arrest on Hogmanay, right in the middle of the party. His health wasn't as it had been, not since his first heart attack. He was now on daily medication, and Grace lived with him to make sure he was alright on a day-to-day basis, after his heart surgery. He had almost died, which was why today was so special to the pair of them and felt a surge of relief and love for his father that he was here on his wedding day.

"Are you feeling nervous, son?" Joe asked as Angus pulled on his suit jacket, and smoothed his hair.

"Aye, I am," Angus laughed. "I dinnae think I was gonnae be today, but I think it's because I have to give a speech."

"Och, it'll be alright, Son," Joe reassured him, patting his shoulder. A high mark of affection as far as Joe, who was stoic at the best of times, was not used to displaying physical affection. "I'm proud of you. You know I felt the same on our wedding day," Joe said,

He looked at Joe with surprise. "You were nervous?"

"Och, of course I was. I couldnae eat, I struggled to sleep the night before, but I'd seen geese flying together that morning, so when I saw your Ma, all the nerves evaporated. She was like a ray on sunshine coming through the clouds when I saw her at the top of the aisle. She looked like an angel, her corn blonde hair loose around her shoulders, a garland of winter roses inter-twined in her hair... Everyone gave a collected gasp of delight. I didnae even feel the cold as she made her way to stand besides me at the head of the aisle…That was braw day," Joe said softly at the memory now, his eyes misty with nostalgia. "The best day of my life, I have to admit."

"Ma used to say she loved a good wedding," he remembered. "Her, The Trinity and Marianne too."

"Aye," Joe agreed. "Cannae beat a good wedding."

"Or a good kipper," Angus added, laughing.

Joe chuckled softly and nodded in agreement. "A braw way to start the day."

"Ma used to say that too," Angus said softly, putting an arm around Joe's shoulders. "I miss her."

"Me too," Joe said softly. "Every day."

He paused, his mind on Annabelle now, holding the memory of her in his mind.

"She was taken from us too soon."

Joe nodded silently, and tried to hide his tears from his son. He didn't need to see him like this on the day of his wedding.

Exhaling slowly, Joe turned to Angus now, his face suddenly serious.

"Son," Joe said, clapping him on his shoulder. "Your Ma would be proud of you. She'd have told you not to be nervous."

"Aye, she would have done…" he replied.

"You remind me of your first day at school. Och, you were so nervous… But then you took your Ma's hand, and I knew you were gonnae be absolutely fine."

He turned Angus to face him now, his voice breaking with emotion. "If you love Eilidh one ounce as much as I loved your Ma, you will be absolutely fine. Just stand up and tell everyone how much you love her. It'll be a great craic. Your gonnae make Eilidh proud. You're gonnae be a grand husband."

"Och, Da," Angus said, noticing there were tears in Joe's eyes. "Are you alright?"

"Aye," Joe said, trying to be his usually stoic self, brushing the tears away with the back of his hand. "I'm so glad you're here today," Angus said, and pulled Joe to him, holding him for a long moment. "I love you, Da."

"Och, I love you too, Son," Joe said, meaning every word. He held him back, and pulled away, looking at him like he was a little boy all over again.

He cleared his throat and checked his watch. "Och, I'm getting sentimental in my old age... Come on, it's almost time. Are you ready to face the music?"

"Aye, I think I am," he replied, nodding, as he straightened his shirt collar, and checked his reflection in the mirror. He looked ruggedly handsome in his kilt, suit jacket and white shirt, dark tousled hair cropped close to his head, beard neatly trimmed.

"Och, and Son," Joe said, turning to him as they together walked to the door. "A word of advice and some would say, the key to a happy marriage."

"Aye?" Angus asked, turning to him now in surprise. He hadn't expected any words of advice today. Joe was not one for words of advice.

"Buy yourselves a dishwasher. I know people don't

often want one, but it frees up your evening, and will be one less thing to argue about."

"Ah, we dinnae really argue," Angus admitted.

"Neither did me and your mother," Joe replied. "She was a ray of sunshine, your Ma. She never had a cross word for anyone. But she often said that was down to having a dishwasher."

Chapter Nineteen

*I*n the bridal suite, Eilidh picked up her veil, admiring the bees and thistles shining in the sunlight streaming through the window as she fixed it in place. She had done her own hair and makeup today, fastening her hair into a neat chignon, fixed with a sprig of white heather.

As she studied her reflection, admiring the way Marianne's dress fit her today, with its gorgeous lace sleeves, and the embroidery along the hem of honeybees.

There was a knock on the door and she opened it to see Robyn, Grace and Connie, and Mhairi and Ollie.

"Aunty Eilidh, you look like a princess!" Mhairi crowed with joy.

"Och, you two look wonderful!"

She welled up at the adorable sight of Mhairi in her ivory bridesmaid dress and flower garland headdress, and Ollie looked smart as well in his navy suit and kilt.

"Och, Eilidh, hen, you look absolutely beautiful,"

Grace gasped, welling up at the sight of her friend, feeling like a proud parent seeing their child at their school play for the first time.

"I love your veil. Was it Marianne's?" Robyn added with a barely conceal sob.

Eilidh nodded, feeling her own eyes well up, and she gave a small sob.

Grace put her arm around her. "Marianne would be so proud of you."

Eilidh nodded and let out a shaky sigh.

"Och, Angus is gonnae be delighted when he sees you," Connie added as there was another knock at the door and the wedding photographer arrived.

"Shall we have a toast?" Connie suggested and everyone nodded, popping the cork on the bottle of champagne she had brought with her.

"To Eilidh and Angus."

The others took a glass and clinked their glasses together.

"To Eilidh and Angus! To True Love!"

"That's wonderful!" The photographer called, and took a few reels of film.

"It's been a long time coming!" Grace said, finishing her champagne, and discreetly noticed out the corner of her eye that Robyn hadn't drunk her's as she wrapped her arm around Eilidh's shoulders, and beamed for the camera.

"I have you and The Trinity to thank for that," Eilidh said, her voice breaking with emotion.

"Aye, we've waited a long time for this," Robyn smiled.

"We dropped enough hints," Grace said. "We thought it wouldnae happen."

"In case you'd forgotten," Eilidh said, with a giggle. "I'd made a vow, swearing off men. I wasnae looking for love."

"And Angus was happy being single, until he saw Eilidh again, and then, Grace sent Angus over to help paint the cottage, and well, the sparks flew!" Robyn added mischievously.

"Aye, well, it helped that it was a hot summer day," Eilidh added, blushing at the memory. "And it helped me make my mind up over my feelings for him."

"And his for you," Connie added.

There was a soft knock on the door and Joe entered the room, followed by Mhairi and Ollie, who looked adorable in their outfits, Mhairi in a gold bridesmaid's dress, and Ollie wearing a navy suit similar to Joe's, with a gold waistcoat.

"Aunty Eilidh, are you ready to go?" Mhairi crowed, rushing into her aunt's arms. "Can we watch you get married yet?"

"Aye, we're almost ready," Eilidh replied, pulling her into a hug. "You look wonderful. I need my bouquet and to put my shoes on…"

"Come on, let's go," Grace smiled, smoothing her

dark green floral tea dress, and taking Mhairi's hand as Robyn helped Eilidh with her train.

"Wait!" Eilidh blurted out as she went to head out of the room, and everyone turned to her. "We cannae go yet. I cannae find my sixpence… its missing from my shoe!"

"What?" Robyn cried, exchanging a look with Grace. "Where was it when you saw it last?"

"I cannae remember," Eilidh cried. "I remember leaving it in my shoe, as Enid said to do, but now it's gone."

"It's alright, hen, we've time to look for it," Connie said, heading into the en-suite and looking for the sixpence.

"Och, am I gonnae get bad luck? I need to find it…" Eilidh cried, looking under the bed frantically.

"Eilidh, Eilidh, listen," Grace said. "Try to keep calm. You're no' gonnae get bad luck. What happened last time isnae gonnae happen again."

Ellidh turned to her, tears welling in her eyes.

"I promise you. Angus is downstairs waiting for you. He's going nowhere without you today."

Eilidh's gave a wobbly sob of relief, and took a deep breath. "I know, I know he wouldnae. If anything we'd better find it before he comes up wondering if I've done a runner."

"Exactly!" Robyn assured her. "Come on, let's look. If you want to have it with you to give you luck, then we will find it."

"Alright," Eilidh replied, letting out a stifled sob.

They all took turns searching the room from top to bottom, looking under the bed, and under the rest of the furniture.

"Look!" Mhairi shouted, and waved a sixpence in the air. "Aunty Eilidh! I found it under the bed. Right in the middle. You cannae see it for all the shadows!"

"Och, thank you, Mhairi!" Eilidh sobbed, taking it from her, and pulling her into a tight hug. "Thank you so much."

She took the sixpence and slipped it inside her shoe.

Everyone gave a collected sigh of relief.

"Come on, hen," Connie said, gently. "Away and fix your makeup."

Eilidh did so and came back a few moments later, looking radiant and composed as Joe arrived.

"You look braw, lass," Joe said, as he took her arm.

Eilidh smiled back, gratefully. "Thank you, for being here, and for agreeing to give me away today."

Eilidh's own father, Hector, had passed away when she was three, and her mother and grandmother had raised her in Mossbrae. She had grown up with Angus, Grace and Robyn, who had been neighbours to Eilidh's late grandmother, Marianne, and now, Eilidh, who had inherited Marianne's cottage, Honeybee Cottage. Her uncle, Fergus had been unable to attend the wedding to give her away as he was on holiday in Australia.

. . .

"Here!" Mhairi cried, handing her the massive bouquet of pink roses, and dark pink heather.

"Thank you," Eilidh said, taking the bouquet in one hand and Joe's arm in the other, and in a second, Grace saw her nerves vanish, replaced by an excited anticipation which was contagious.

"Come on, show time..." Robyn announced and took Eilidh's train. "We want to get to the good bit!"

"Ready?" Joe asked Eilidh, and she nodded. "Come on, then. Time to get you down that aisle!"

Chapter Twenty

*A*s Grace and Robyn made their way into the drawing room which was acting as the ceremony room today, Grace's shoes tapping across the dark oak hardwood floor. The room was decorated with the late Georgian features, looking wonderful today. It was a large drawing room with a massive chandelier in the centre, and two walls were windows, offering a gorgeous scenic views of the gardens and the rest of the estate. Rory's team had decorated it beautifully, with white and pink balloons and gold chairs decorated with pink and white ribbons to seat the congregation.

The opening strains of Vivaldi's Spring struck up, as Grace made her way down the aisle, admiring the rest of the congregation, and found her seat in the centre row next to Paul. Enid was wearing black and white, Maudie, light pink floral which matched her candyfloss pink hair, and Nelly was wearing a cream dress with a sunflower print, to match her sunny nature.

"Och, look at Angus!" Grace murmured to Paul, choking back tears of sheer happiness. Her gaze turned to Angus now, who was standing at the head of the aisle, looking nervous.

Glancing over her shoulder as the Mendelssohn wedding march struck up, Grace felt tears welling in her eyes as Eilidh entered the room on Joe's arm, followed by a beaming Mhairi, and jubilant Ollie.

"Och, look at Angus! He hasnae cried like that since he was about ten and he lambed his first lamb."

She gestured to Angus, who had tears running down his cheeks at the mere sight of his bride-to-be.

Eilidh reached the head of the aisle, and letting go of Joe's arm, as he led the kids to join Grace and Paul, then turned to face Angus, ready to change her life forever.

"Och, she loves so beautiful!" Maudie gasped, as she held back a sob. "And look at the bairns!"

"She's a vision and so are they," Enid agreed, with a nod, and that made Grace smile even more, given Enid was no one who showed her emotions.

"And, she's wearing that veil that Marianne gave her," Nelly murmured, wiping her eyes.

"She looks so pretty!" Mhairi whispered excitedly.

"She looks braw," Joe murmured, smiling over as Eilidh and Angus exchanged a glance of pure happiness.

Grace saw him mouth his appreciation, as Eilidh reached him, and handed her bouquet to Robyn, who took her place besides Orion behind Grace and Paul.

The redheaded registrar, hired especially for the day by Rory and Isla, with a warm smile as she began the ceremony.

"Ladies and gentlemen," she announced, as she began the ceremony. "We are gathered here today to celebrate the wedding of Eilidh and Angus. They have decided to write their own vows. But, before we begin, are there any objections?"

The congregation remained silent.

"I guess that settles it. So shall we begin?"

"I'm so nervous!" Eilidh giggled, as the attention fell on them.

"Angus, would you like to go first?"

Angus cleared this throat, and took her hand in his.

"Eilidh, we're standing here promising to love each other forever, and I plan to do that today. Eilidh, I've loved you since we first met in a lambing shed at the age of three and five. I knew we were destined to be together, and I just had to wait until you realised you felt the same, because I saw all the signs were there that you liked me back."

Eilidh beamed up at him, her eyes shining with tears.

"I adore you, so very much. I cannae wait to spend our lives together, to build our lives, and our legacy, and most of all, to be happy, because you make me the happiest man in the world."

With that, he reached for her hand, and slid the ring onto her finger. "Now, and forever."

Eilidh glanced at everyone to see there wasn't a dry eye in the entire congregation.

"Eilidh, now it's your turn," The registrar said, and Eilidh glanced down at her ring, then back up at Angus's handsome, waiting face.

"Angus, we're standing here promising to love each other forever, and I plan to do that today. In truth, I didn't dare dream that this day would come, as for so many years, we were only friends."

They smiled at each other.

"I had made a vow, not to get my heart broken, because I was grieving, but you were there for me. You supported me, and you were my best friend. You brought me the beehives and helped reignite my passion. But I didnae dare admit your kindness meant more than being a good friend. Little did I know...And then the light dawned when we painted the cottage together."

Everyone gave a soft knowing chuckle, and The Trinity and Grace and Robyn shared a congratulatory look.

"I realised I adored you, and I wanted more than anything to be with you."

Angus's face crumpled into an emotional smile.

"When you proposed in our back garden on a hot summer's day, and all my dreams came true. And, now, here we are, and I swear I'm going to spend the rest of my life trying to make you as happy as you make me. You're my best friend, my love, and there is no-one I want to spend the rest of my life with."

Eilidh sniffed, and smiled at him through a sheen of tears.

"From today, we are joined as one, a team, and we build our future together, the cottage, the honey business, the farm, and we will be family. I love you more than I ever, forever..."

The registrar handed her the ring and she took Angus's hand and slid the ring onto his wedding finger.

"Congratulations, you are officially, man and wife," the registrar, turning to Angus with a grin. "You may kiss the bride!"

Everyone cheered, as Angus took Eilidh in his arms and kissed her passionately.

"Och! So romantic!" Maudie sighed, dabbing her eyes with a handkerchief, her nose and cheeks as pink as her candy-floss pink hair. "They've finally done it!"

There was a huge cheer and several rounds of applause and Eilidh and Angus grinned at each other like teenagers, before Angus took her hand, and they walked back down the aisle to Ode to Joy.

"That was the best wedding I've ever been to," Maudie announced, dabbing her eyes as the followed the rest of the congregation out into the front of the house, to have the photos taken.

"Aye, it's a long time coming but they'll have a long and happy marriage," Enid agreed.

Maudie gave Enid a conspiratorial sideways glance.

"I think we need to have another match made," Maudie announced.

"Aye, we still need to find a match for Dougie," Enid asked.

Grace couldn't help but smile as she glanced at Paul. "The Trinity are at it again. Wondering who they can match next."

"They are good at it though," Paul replied, putting an arm around her. "Look at us. We've my Granny to thank for us meeting, aye?"

"Aye," Grace replied with a smile. "We have. We have to admit, grannies have a gift for matchmaking…"

Chapter Twenty-One

he Past.

Aviemore

"Grace, come out," Archie called as he banged on the bathroom door. "Grace! Will you stop being dramatic?"

"I'm no' being dramatic," Grace replied as she opened the door, face red with fury. "How long have you been messing around with Clara?"

It was the week after Joe and Annabelle's anniversary and Grace and Archie were back in Aviemore. Things however, weren't going well. That morning, Grace had found incriminating texts to from Clara on Archie's phone, another student on their course.

"Oh, come on, we're all on the same course. We're

not seeing each other," Archie replied, but something in his gaze made her suspicious.

"Why have you been secretly texting her then?"

"It isn't a secret. We're just friends."

"I dinnae believe you," Grace replied, and brushed past him, heading for the door.

"I'm sorry, alright? I'll make it up to you tonight? We'll go to that new Italian place."

"We'll see. I have to get to work," Grace said coolly, thinking on Enid's words at her parent's wedding anniversary.

For this term, the students were on placement, and for Grace and Archie, it was at the Grouse and Thistle, in Aviemore. Grace was really enjoying it, and felt she was coming into her own as a trainee chef. Glancing up at the clock at the end of her busy shift, she was doing a double shift, she sighed with relief to see it was almost four pm. She couldn't wait to head home, shower, change out of her sweaty clothes and have a well-earned rest.

"See you first thing tomorrow, Grace," Gregor, the head chef said, as he closed up the kitchen, and she nodded, heading out of the front door, and almost tripping over a young man who was about her age who was stood next to the door.

"Och! Sorry!" The young man cried.

"Can I help you?" Grace asked, glancing up at him.

He towered over her at nearly six foot tall, but she could see from here he was handsome, with red hair and bright blue eyes.

"Yes, please. I was waiting for you, actually."

"Me?" Grace asked, with a double take.

"Aye. I was in earlier with my grandmother for her birthday, and we ordered the roast lamb. I wanted to say it was magnificent."

"Thank you," Grace replied, looking at him now. He was well dressed, wearing a pale blue polo shirt and jeans. He was clean shaven, and had a boyish charm to him that made her suddenly wish she wasn't sweaty from her shift, dirty haired, and wearing hardly any makeup.

"Have you finished your shift?" The young man asked and she nodded.

"Aye, I am just away home."

"Ah, right," he said, looking a little awkward, and she wondered what he wanted. He didn't look like a creep though and she didn't feel unsafe, but she wasn't used to strange men waiting for her outside of work.

"Sorry," he said. "Um, I didnae meant to come across as weird...I dinnae usually do this...I'm Paul."

He offered his hand, and she shook it.

"Grace."

"Are you alright, Son? Can we help you with anything?" Gregor asked as he locked up.

"Aye, I'm good, thank you, I um... I was just talking to Grace."

"He bothering you, hen?" Gregor asked.

"No. He's harmless," Grace replied, with a smile.

"Ask her out then, Son. The poor lass has had a busy shift. Treat her to a nice meal…"

Paul blushed to the roots of his hair, as Grace turned to him in surprise. Looking up at Paul now, Grace realised that he really was quite handsome. There was something appealing about his light blue eyes. She saw a kindness there. Something told her he would make a good friend. She pushed the thought of Archie and Clara to one side. They could go out as friends, couldn't they? Archie couldn't stop her having a new friend.

"You wanted to ask me out? On a date?"

"Aye, that was the plan, but I'm not very good at this, I'm sorry…Would you like to go for a drink some time?"

Then, she shook her head. "Look, I'll be honest with you, I'm seeing someone right now, so I'm not looking for romance. But I would like another friend."

"Ah, well, that wouldnae be an issue," Paul replied. "Are you free tomorrow night? What time do you finish your shift?"

"I finish at midday. I'm on a morning shift tomorrow. Shall I meet you here then?"

"Aye, that would be grand," Paul replied, his face lighting up and Grace smiled. He seemed like he would be a good friend. Grace nodded, and she liked his boyish grin. And as he walked away to his car, she realised she was looking forward to having a new friend.

~

The following afternoon, Grace met Paul in the centre of Aviemore, wearing her black wool coat and a new peacock blue shift dress with knee boots to keep her legs warm from the cold. She liked to dress up when she went out and it felt nice to do her hair and put on some makeup.

"Hello," Paul called as he saw her approach, and she was surprised to feel her heart race a little faster at the sight of him.

"Hello!"

"You look lovely. Shall we head off?"

With a nod, she followed him towards his car.

"Grace!"

She turned at the sound of her name and swore under her breath at the sight of Archie who had turned up to begin his shift. and her heart sank to see he was holding a bunch of flowers.

"Are they for Clara?" She asked, nodding to the flowers.

"No," Archie said, looking genuinely hurt. "They're for you. To apologise."

"I'm busy at the moment. Can we talk later?"

"Where are you going?" Archie demanded after her shift as she changed into her new peacock-blue dress and heels. "Why are you dressed up?"

"I'm having dinner with a friend."

"Is that what you call it?"

"That's what you call it when you're seeing Clara,"

Grace said airily, and climbed into the car, slamming the door.

"Is everything alright?" Paul asked, as he glanced across at the puce faced Archie.

"Aye, everything is fine," Grace replied, as they drove out of the car park.

"Is that the boyfriend?"

"Aye, it is. I'm sorry about him. He's been cheating with a girl called Clara."

"Ah, I'm sorry." Paul said sympathetically.

"Forget about him now," Grace glanced over at him, curiosity peaked. "So were are we going for lunch?"

"Ah," Paul said, his face lighting up with a grin. "I have a surprise for you."

"Och! Is this the new gastro pub, The Runaway Haggis? I've heard lots of recommendations!" Grace gasped, as they drove into the centre of Aviemore. "I've wanted to come here for ages!"

"Aye, I thought you might like it," Paul replied. "Shall we head in? They have a special lunch menu."

They walked inside the busy, bright, airy restaurant, which was chicly decorated, and had hardwood floors throughout, with traditional pipe music playing quietly in the background.

"They do traditional food, but with a twist, apparently," he added as the matre'd were shown to a table.

"Och, I cannae wait to try it out," Grace said

admiring the decor, and seeing Ardeverikie House in the distance through the window.

"Och! Look at the view!" she cried, trying not to shriek with delight.

"The menu's no' bad either," Paul said with a grin.

"What shall we have to start?" Grace asked. "The langoustines are caught fresh daily apparently and shipped from Newhaven."

"Is that so?"

Paul nodded, pleased to see how impressed she was.

For starters, they ordered scallops baked in the shell, with lobster to follow with garlic butter, fries, and heather cream liquor flavoured ice cream to finish.

"So what got you into catering?" Paul asked as they waited for the starters.

"I've always loved cooking. I used to bake with my mother as a child. We grew up on a hill farm but I didnae want a career in farming."

"I'd love to have grown up on a farm, always outdoors in the fresh air," Paul replied. "I grew up in the city."

"Aye?" She asked, remembering Joe's words about city boys.

"Aye, dinnae hold it against me though, I'd gladly swap with you," Paul joked. "What's your favourite thing to cook?"

"Cakes. I love doing all the decorating, icing, sprinkles, the lot. All the details are so much fun," Grace replied, and he smiled at her enthusiasm. "What about you?"

"I'm afraid I'm no' much of a chef," Paul admitted. "Though I've been told I'm good at DIY."

"Aye? Putting up fences and that kind of thing?" Grace asked.

"I built a chimney once," Paul replied, and Grace liked how proud he sounded. "If I wasnae in I.T. I wanted to be a builder."

"Aye? What made you head into I.T.?"

"I love computing. I set up websites now," Paul explained as their starters arrived and the scent of garlic and lemon made their mouths water.

Grace gasped, as they tucked in. She hadn't eaten such delicious food for a long time.

"These are braw!"

Paul chuckled at her enthusiasm. "Oh, you have a wee bit of butter…"

He reached out a thumb and wiped the butter away, making her blush.

"Thank you," she murmured, her gaze meeting his. He really was handsome, that red hair, the blue eyes, boyish but charming with it. He smiled back, as he enjoyed his starter.

Grace found herself looking at him for a moment too long, and blushing, looked away. She shouldn't be thinking of him like that. They'd only just met last night, and she wasn't one for jumping from boyfriend to boyfriend, but there was something intriguing and exciting about Paul.

The mains came, and Grace almost gasped at the sight of the lobster, surrounded by fries, and the mouth watering scent of garlic butter wafting up to meet them.

"Now that looks braw!" Paul exclaimed, and rubbed his hands together with glee as the plates were placed in front of them.

The mains were even better than the starters. The flavours of garlic, lemon, and lime alongside the meaty texture of the lobster creating a melting pot of flavours in her mouth, and the fries were crispy, deliciously crunchy, and before too long, it was over and they looked down at spotless plates.

"That. Was. Amazing," Grace said, beaming up at him. "All I can do is thank you for bringing me here."

"You're most welcome," Paul grinned. "Nothing like a delicious meal."

"And braw company," Grace added.

"I'm glad you're having a good time," Paul said, his gaze meeting hers. "Wait until you've had the pudding though."

Grace nodded, as their plates were taken away, and their pudding came.

"This," Grace said with childish enthusiasm. "Is the kind of pudding I want to make people. The flavours are wonderful!"

"Aye, whisky is always a winner."

"Och, you can say that again!"

They smiled at each other, and finished their meal.

"That was amazing," Grace announced when they finished and they paid the bill.

"I'm glad you enjoyed it," Paul said as they left the

restaurant and out into the mild winter afternoon. "Would you like to do this again? As friends, I mean."

"Aye, I would," Grace replied, nodding. "I'd love to do that."

And she realised she couldn't wait to see him again.

Chapter Twenty-Two

he Past.

Three Weeks Later.

"Are you alright, Ma?" Grace asked softly as she glanced across at Annabelle as they sat in the doctor's now.

"Hmm? Aye, I'm alright, hen, dinnae fret," Annabelle murmured, focusing on the rain outside. It was mid January, and finally, thanks to the Christmas and Hogmanay holidays, had managed to get a doctor's appointment. The doctor's in Mossbrae was part of the General Infirmary, with a small building attached to the main hospital where people could go and see a GP for non-emergency appointments.

"Shall I get you some water whilst we're waiting?"

Grace asked, trying to stem her own anxiety at being here, and help notice that she was looking pale today, her corn blonde hair looking dark against her cheekbones, even in her vibrant pink jumper and jeans.

Annabelle shook her head. "I'll get called in a moment."

"Mrs. Kincaid?" Dr. Smith, a prim looking lady dressed in a tweed skirt suit, called from her consultation room, and Annabelle stood, gesturing to Grace.

"Can my daughter come with me?"

The doctor nodded and they went into the room and sat down on stiff blue plastic chairs which reminded Grace of being at primary school as she watched and quietly listened.

"So you've come today with pains in your side? How often are you getting these pains?" Doctor Smith asked in gentle, dulcet tones.

Annabelle nodded. "Every other day. I have been for the past few weeks."

"Any other symptoms?"

"Head aches, sickness, and dizziness," Annabelle replied, ticking the points off her fingers. "I've also found a lump..."

"What?" Grace gasped in alarm, visibly paling. "Och, Ma, you never said..."

"I didnae want to worry any of you," Annabelle continued, putting a hand on her arm.

"It's in my armpit," she continued, addressing Dr.

Smith, who nodded seriously.

"Let's check you... can you slip your arm out of your sleeve?"

Annabelle did so as the doctor checked her.

"There is a lump there. It's quite small, but I think we should send you for a biopsy regardless."

Grace paled further, glancing at Annabelle who seemed quite calm. "A biopsy?"

"Yes. We will be able to tell whether then the lump is cancerous or not."

"Do you think it is cancerous?"

"I'm afraid it's impossible to tell just by sight. I'll book you a referral to the oncology department now. It shouldn't be too long for you to get an appointment."

Annabelle nodded, and Grace took her hand and squeezed it as she struggled to process everything.

"How long will it take for the results?" Annabelle asked, impassively.

"About three weeks. We're lucky there is a fast turn around with us being so close to the hospital."

Doctor Smith smiled at her gently once she had finished typing on the computer. "You should get your appointment soon, and then we can find out."

"Thank you," Annabelle replied as she pulled her coat back on.

"Take care," Doctor Smith called and they exchanged pensive smile.

"Dinnae fret, Ma," Grace said firmly as she took her arm and lead her back to the car. "I'll stay with you until you have an appointment."

"Gracie, hen," Annabelle turned to face her. "I want you to go back to Aviemore."

"But you need me."

"There's nothing we can do until I get my appointment, so you're best off at college. It will help distract you."

"Och, Ma!" Grace cried and flung her arms around her. "I love you."

"I love you too, hen. Never forget that."

Six weeks later

It was a mild early March morning, and as she came home from college, Grace remembered exactly where she was when the news of the biopsy came in the post. Joe and Angus were out with the ewes, awaiting the scanner when the post came.

Three weeks ago, Annabelle had had to stay overnight and have a biopsy on the lump under her arm, whilst Marianne had helped Joe take care of the kids and dogs.

"Ma?" Grace said, glancing between her mother and the letter.

The tension was palpable as she watched her hold the letter calmly, hesitating to open it which made her want to snatch it off her, tear it open and break the tension.

The doorbell rang, and Annabelle glanced up, breaking the spell.

"Annabelle, hello hen!" Marianne called, as she opened the door.

Then, she saw the letter in her hand. "Have you opened it yet?"

"No," Annabelle replied.

"Right, let's get a brew," Marianne replied, putting her arm around her, and lead them into the kitchen. "Hello, Gracie, hen. I brought some more lavender honey round."

"I was gonnae make shortbread," Annabelle murmured, all attention on the letter in her hand.

"Have a seat," Marianne encouraged gently as she moved to the kettle and made tea. Tea solved everything.

Once the tea was made, she placed the cup in front of her, and sat opposite her.

"Here you are hen. You've gone pale."

Annabelle glanced up at her.

"I think it's time, hen. Open the letter."

Grace took a seat next to Annabelle, and sat down, feeling her heart pounding in her chest, so loudly she could hear the blood rushing in her ears.

With a slow exhalation, Annabelle opened the letter and read it, clapping a hand over her mouth to silence the noisy sobs a few seconds later.

"Ma?" Grace asked, leaning forward, and throwing her arms around her, tears springing to her own eyes. "I'm here, Ma."

There was the click of a key in the doorway and Joe and Angus came back from dealing with the sheep.

"Any news?" Joe asked and then saw the scene at the dining table. "Ah…"

He moved across the room and took her in his arms. "It's alright hen, I'm here. We all are."

Annabelle sniffed, burying her head in his shoulder. Out of the pair of them, Joe was the stronger one, the one who could deal with things when they cropped up. Also, he had the farm to run, their legacy to keep afloat, and she knew this news would break it, threaten to ruin everything.

"I've got stage three cancer," Annabelle murmured, her voice breaking as she handed the letter to him.

Joe read it, and she saw the heartbreak in his eyes. "Och, hen, I'm so sorry."

Annabelle let out a sob and shushing her, Joe rocked her in his arms.

Grace sat, watching the scene and feeling numb with shock. Marianne moved to her and put a maternal arm around her and Angus. She dabbed her eyes, hit by a sudden wave of grief that she might lose her best friend.

Annabelle sat back down and took a sip of tea.

"I have a follow up hospital appointment tomorrow."

"I'll come with you!" Grace blurted but Annabelle shook her head.

"You need to head back tomorrow."

"I'm staying," Grace replied as she rushed to her side. "I cannae go back now."

"Hen," Annabelle said, taking her in her arms. "I need you to. Da can come with me."

"Aye, of course."

"I can take care of everything," Angus added, ever practical.

Grace looked at them and nodded, feeling bereft.

"I'll call you as soon as we've spoken to the oncologist."

Grace nodded, trying to be strong, not only for Annabelle, but for all of them.

It was quiet in the hospital the following morning as Annabelle and Joe waited for to be called in.

"It's taking ages," Annabelle murmured as he held her hand.

"It's only been ten minutes hen."

"Where is everyone?"

She glanced around at the near empty room, and shivered despite it being warm to the point of being cosy.

"Mrs Kincaid? This way, please," called a pleasant looking nurse who lead them down the corridor.

"Time to face the music," Annabelle let out a long sigh, and hesitated. "Do I look alright?" She asked, uncertainly.

"Aye," Joe replied, taking in her bright pink coat. "You look beautiful."

They followed her into the consultation room.

"Good morning," said the doctor. "I'm Doctor McKinnon."

Doctor McKinnon was an older lady, with steel grey hair, and bright blue eyes. "We're here today to discuss your results, and where we can go from here. I see you've received the letter."

"I have," Annabelle replied numbly. "What are my options?"

"Well, the biopsy revealed the lump is cancerous. It is stage three cancer, meaning it has spread to the lymph nodes in your under arm."

Doctor McKinnon glanced up at her. "The good news is that not many of the lymph nodes have been affected. This means we can treat it."

"That's a relief!" Joe replied, patting Annabelle's arm.

"What sort of treatment can I receive?" Annabelle asked.

"We are going to try radiotherapy, which we are hopeful will shrink the tumour."

Annabelle nodded, silently.

"We think that it will take about three months of an intensive course. We'll start next week and see how it goes. I'll arrange a follow up appointment for you."

"Thank you," Annabelle replied, feeling a little glimmer of hope in the gloom.

Chapter Twenty-Three

"Where are Grace and Paul?" Robyn asked as the congregation headed outside to take photos.

"Are you alright?" Orion asked her as they headed outside to the minibus, ready to drive through the estate for the photos.

"Aye, I'm fine," she said, tucking a stray hair behind her ear.

"Are you sure?" Orion asked, bending his head to her.

"Actually, I have something to tell you."

She looked up at him, and tugging his hand, lead him back into the house. "It's really important. I dinnae want anyone to overhear us…"

"Well, you're making it a bit obvious something is up with us sneaking away like this," Orion replied, putting a hand on her arm.

"I'm fine," Robyn assured him as they went into the

kitchens, and she closed the door behind them. "I'm three weeks pregnant."

Orion's eyes widened with shock. "Really?"

"I've taken a test, look," Robyn took the test from her handbag and showed him.

"I cannae believe it," Orion whispered, taking it from her and marvelling at it. Then he took her in his arms and kissed her, as she did, she felt the wetness of tears on his cheek.

"Are you crying?" she whispered, raising a hand and stroking his cheek, feeling her own cheeks wet with tears.

"No," he said unconvincingly, his face crumpling with emotion, and he let out a ragged breath, his voice breaking with emotion. "I cannae believe it. We're gonnae get a second chance at this."

"It's true," she said, her own voice breaking as he took her in his arms. "I cannae believe it either."

"I love you so much, Robyn."

"I love you too," she replied as he held her tightly, and then he gave a soft chuckle. "I thought there was something up."

"Really?" Robyn asked, looking up at him. "Was it the kippers?"

Orion nodded, and she giggled. "I think they gave you away. In fact, I think everyone has guessed already."

"I think you're right," Robyn replied, smiling. "Enid said something about surprises on the minibus."

"Aye? Well, if they already know, why are we

standing here and not talking about this on the minibus?"

"I case they dinnae know," Robyn replied. "It's Eilidh and Angus's big day!"

"Alright, we'll keep it quiet. For now," Orion replied. "I want to shout it from the rooftops and keep it secret until the baby arrives all at the same time."

Robyn nodded in agreement. "I know what you mean…I've never felt so excited, and scared."

"It willnae happen again," Orion said, stroking her cheek. "I promise."

"But you cannae promise something like that," Robyn shook her head. "We have to take it a day at a time."

"Aye, we do, and we will," he placed a hand on her stomach protectively. "But everything will be fine."

Then, Orion's expression changed to one of mild confusion.

"Can I smell a cake baking?"

"Aye, dinnae ask. It's a long story," Robyn chuckled and took his hand. "Come on, let's get back to the minibus…"

"There you are !" Maudie called cheerfully as they rejoined the group outside. "We're all waiting! Where have you two been?"

"Oh, just talking," Robyn replied, tucking a hair behind her ear.

Maudie gave her a knowing look but didn't say any more, as they followed everyone across the gravel towards the minibus.

They drove to the rose gardens and soon, everyone was enveloped in the heady scent of roses.

"Shall we do the confetti first?"

Everyone moved to form an arch, and holding hands, Eilidh and Angus held hands and walked through as the confetti was handed out. Mhairi threw it with a squeal, as she threw the pink, white and purple confetti over Angus and Eilidh who laughed in delight, as they were showered with petals as the congregation cheered.

"Cheers!" Angus said, clinking his glass against Eilidh's. "Here's to you, Mrs. Kincaid."

Eilidh smiled back at him, her eyes wet with tears. "I cannae believe that we've finally done it!"

She waggled her fingers, admiring her wedding ring. Angus grinned back. "I love you, Paddington."

"I love you."

Their gaze met, and he pulled her to him in a kiss that made her head spin. It felt for a moment as though everyone disappeared, leaving just the two of them.

Then came the photos.

"Shall we do the bridal party first?" asked the photographer, and Eilidh nodded, ushering Robyn, Grace, Connie, and The Trinity to her, and they beamed as the photographer took a plethora of photos.

"Wonderful! Let's get the groomsmen now."

Joe, Paul, Rory and Orion stepped forward, with Cedric on the end.

"Och, it's been a braw wedding," Maudie commented to Grace as they watched and she nodded, as bucks fizz was handed out "Everything is going to plan..."

"Aye."

Grace glanced at Cedric, and then back to Enid.

"I was thinking, what we need, is a wee bit of matchmaking. After all, in order to face the future, we need to face our past..."

Enid nodded and glanced across at Cedric.

"Aye, we do. But whom?"

"Leanna was saying Rhona gets lonely but she daren't admit it, filling her days with work to take her mind off it," Grace replied lightly.

"A wonderful idea!" Maudie gasped in delight.

"Congratulations! Mrs Kincaid!" Nelly exclaimed as The Trinity as they walked over and clinked glasses with her and Grace.

"Thanks," Eilidh grinned.

"It was a gorgeous ceremony," Maudie sighed. "The best wedding we've been to for years. The wedding of the year!"

"I agree," Angus grinned, putting his arm around Eilidh's shoulders and gave her a look of pure love.

Even Enid, who was most stoic of the three sisters, shed a tear.

"Congratulations!" Grace announced as she hugged Eilidh warmly as The Trinity and Angus went to mingle.

"I'm so glad you're here," Eilidh replied, feeling her heart surge with emotion. "Thank you for making it a wonderful day. I cannae wait for the cake… I swear I could smell it earlier…"

"Really? I didnae smell anything," Grace replied, adding with a covert smile, "they do say, your senses are heightened…when you're pregnant…"

She glanced at her pointedly, looking for a tell-tale glimmer in Eilidh's eyes, but she looked at her in bemusement.

"Aye, is that so?"

"Have you told Angus yet?" Grace asked, barely able to conceal her own excitement. "Dinnae fret, I'll keep quiet…"

"Told Angus what?" She asked, lowering her voice to a whisper.

"About…" Grace gave a discreet glance.

"But I'm no' pregnant."

Grace looked at her in confusion, and then they glanced over at Robyn, who was chatting with Maudie.

"You dinnae think?" Eilidh asked, and Grace shrugged, feeling her heart surge with love.

"I really hope so…" she said, crossing her fingers discreetly.

· · ·

"Let's have one of everyone now!"

"Come on," Eilidh said, tugging Grace's hand, and they lined up with everyone else.

"Take you back, aye?" Paul whispered to her as he put an arm around her shoulders.

"Aye," Grace said fondly, glancing back at him. "It does. Everyone knew you were The One long before we got together. I'm so glad we met…"

"Aye, me too," Paul grinned, pressing his mouth to her's in a gentle kiss.

Chapter Twenty-four

he Past

Summer

The air was still and humid as the music from the top field drifted across from the CD player at Cairnmhor Farm. It was Joe's birthday, and Annabelle had organised a party held in the field behind the farmhouse. She had been planning it for weeks, and was looking forward to seeing Joe's face when she presented him with what she had planned.

Joe followed Grace and Robyn brought the food out into the early afternoon sunlight, and laid it out on the wrought iron table near the edge of the field in the shade of the trees, laying out wrought iron chairs, and Annabelle followed them with the birthday cake as The Trinity arrived.

Maudie was wearing a light candy floss pink sundress and hat, which matched her hair. Enid, bespectacled and stoic had opted for a sensible cream shift dress, and Nelly was wearing a bright yellow dress and matching sandals, her long hair tied back in a ponytail.

"Hello!" She called. "Happy Birthday, Joe!"

"Hello!" Joe called back. "Thank you, how lovely to see you all. How are you?"

"Och, we're braw," Enid replied, as she handed over his birthday present.

"Thank you," said Joe, and Maudie settled herself into a chair with a contented sigh.

"This is a braw set up and it's lovely to see everyone!"

"It's wonderful to see you again. It's been too long!" Grace said brightly.

"Aye. it has! How is college? Are you enjoying it?"

"Aye, I am. I'm learning a lot. I've been learning how to make bread, cakes and we're learning how to make pastry."

"Och, it sounds like time well spent!" Nelly agreed and she nodded.

"I've having a grand time. I made the cake today. I cannae wait for you to see it."

"What's the plan afterwards?"

"I want to open my own bakery." Grace replied, proudly.

"Och, that's a grand idea! I hope you do well," Enid said. "It'll happen, you just need to be patient."

Grace held her gaze and knew she was right.

"And you'll get to meet my friend, Paul today too. He's coming along shortly."

"Aye, your friend?" Maudie asked, looking delighted at another opportunity to matchmake.

"Turn the music up!" Robyn called as she set out a jug of home made lemonade and glasses.

"Have we got enough chicken thighs?" Grace asked Joe.

"Och, that looks grand!" Joe called, glancing over at the table, which was laid with a variety of delicious food. Grace had come home specially, with a whole array of food she had prepared for the party. Grace had made mini venison pies, ham lattice, pesto pasta, potato salad, and smoked salmon quiche, vegetarian rice salad, mini venison pies with red wine gravy, Annabelle's rosemary and thyme dumplings, and her favourite part, the birthday cake.

"Especially the cake! Gracie, you've done a wonderful job!" Annabelle announced, carrying it out with a grin. It looked wonderful, a square cake covered in green icing, with rolled icing sheep, and a mini quad bike next to a mini lambing shed.

Grace blushed. She had been practicing her cake baking, and had spend hours practicing how to work rolled icing, and she found she was wonderful at it. She had been practicing how to make rolled icing sheep, and now had a little flock of them. It had taken several attempts, but Grace thought she had finally got it.

"Aye! That's a braw cake!" Robyn exclaimed, shading her eyes in the bright afternoon sunlight.

"Och, that course has done wonders!" Maudie, sitting in a deck chair opposite. "I cannae wait to try everything!"

"Aye, that smoked salmon quiche is calling my name!" Nelly announced, and Enid, who was sitting in the shade, nodded quietly.

"Can we start eating now?" Robyn asked.

"No, wait a moment," Annabelle chided gently. "It's your Da's birthday, and we're waiting for Paul."

"Oh aye, I forgot Grace's new boyfriend is coming today. What time is he getting here?"

"He's on his way in a taxi now," Grace replied. "And he's not my boyfriend."

"Yet," said Maudie with a grin. "Och, from what we've heard, he sounds like a good potential boyfriend…"

Grace shook her head, smiling. "I'm still seeing Archie."

Joe exchanged a look with Annabelle, who shrugged.

After that disastrous meeting at Christmas, things had cooled between the pair, but from what Annabelle had reported, they were still dating, although more casually than before, and as far as she knew, he wasn't cheating on her any more.

"Dinnae fret," Maudie whispered to Annabelle. "She'll see sense once Paul arrives..."

Having seen photos of Paul, Annabelle had seen potential there. He was handsome and from what Grace had reported, he was shaping up to be a great friend.

"Friendship is a solid foundation for a relationship," Nelly said pointedly.

Grace smiled sweetly, and turned her attention to the drive as Marianne and Eilidh arrived.

"Hello!" Marianne called over, a birthday present tucked under her arm. "Happy birthday, Joe!"

"Och, that's too kind, Marianne," Joe said, as he greeted her warmly. "Come and have some food."

"Hello," Eilidh called shyly, and Robyn rushed to her and hugged her warmly. "Come and look at the cake. Grace made it, and it's braw!"

Eilidh and Robyn went to admire the cake.

"Where's Angus?" Marianne asked, as she took a seat next to the Trinity. "Och, it's a gorgeous day for a birthday, aye?"

"It is. He's on his way," Joe said. "He said he wanted to check the lambs afore he joined us."

"Eilidh will be pleased to hear that," Robyn said with a cheeky wink, as she took a couple of chicken thighs and wiped her fingers on her purple t-shirt.

"Robyn! Manners!" Annabelle chided, handing her a paper serviette.

"Thank you," Robyn said automatically. "Och, there are braw! Well done, Gracie!"

Grace, dressed in a lime green dress, an emerald ribbon fastened into her hair, reminding Eilidh of Mariette Larkin from the Darling Buds of May, with her dark curly hair and ruddy outdoorsy complexion. At twenty-four, she was only three years older than Eilidh and Robyn, but she had always seemed more mature, like a mini mother to them all.

"Hullo!"

They looked up and saw Angus striding across the field, followed by the dogs, who were wagging their tales with excitement.

"Hello!" Eilidh called back with a grin, and The Trinity smiled and exchanged a glance with Marianne to see her discreetly smooth her orange strappy sundress.

If ever a girl had a crush, it was obvious, she had one on Angus. They glanced over at Angus, judging his reaction.

"It's great to see you," Angus said, putting his am around her. "How have you been?"

"I've been admiring the birthday cake."

"Aye, it's braw. Gracie's done a grand job. Can we get started yet?"

"No, Paul isnae here yet," Grace was saying just as the taxi arrived and he got out and waved.

"Hello!" he called, heading towards them across the

field, and handed Joe a carefully wrapped present when he reached them.

"Happy birthday, Mr. Kincaid."

"Thank you," said Joe with a smile, liking him already as he opened it to find a bottle of his favourite whisky. "Och, this is grand. Call me Joe."

"Alright. I'm Paul."

Joe took in the tall redheaded young man before him, wearing a dark green polo shirt and jeans and trainers, and liked him immediately. He seemed polite and didn't have that arrogance Archie had had.

Grace introduced him to everyone.

"And this, is Paul."

"It's a pleasure to finally meet you," Annabelle said, reaching for his hand. "Grace has told us a lot about you."

"All good I hope," Paul joked, and then looked around. "It's a braw farm. I love hearing the sound of the sheep bleating. I've always wanted to live on a farm."

"Aye?" Maudie said, glancing at Annabelle hopefully. "Well, maybe Gracie can give you a wee tour later…"

"Aye, I'd like that," Paul said enthusiastically, looking at Grace hopefully.

"Aye, go on then," Grace agreed. She stepped forward with a plate and began loading it up with food.

"Da, what do you want to eat?"

"A bit of everything please, hen," Joe said, and Grace handed him a plate.

"Thanks hen," he said, carrying the plate to the table, and they all gathered around to eat.

"This is delicious," Paul said, as he finished another chicken thigh. "Is this paprika and lemon?"

Grace nodded proudly. "It's a new recipe."

"It's fantastic."

They smiled at each and Marianne gave Annabelle an encouraging nudge. Annabelle nodded in agreement.

Joe turned to Annabelle as he observed them chatting happily.

"He seems nice," he said, nodding over to Paul, liking how he was making Grace laugh. "Seems like a nice guy."

"Aye, and he and Grace are getting on well. It's promising to say the least."

"She just needs to get rid of the other one…"

Annabelle put a gentle hand on his arm. "She'll see the light in her own time."

Joe nodded begrudgingly, and finished his food.

"I think it's time for the cake!"

Annabelle stood and added the candles to the cake and started the opening bars of Happy Birthday.

Everyone joined in, raising their glasses of home made lemonade in a toast.

"To Joe. Happy Birthday!"

"Speech!" Robyn called and Joe reluctantly stood up.

"Alright, I'll give a wee speech… Thank you all for

coming. It's been wonderful to have the whole family back together plus some brilliant extras. Hope to see you again in the future, aye?"

He winked at Grace who let out a soft chuckle, and Paul patted her shoulder good-naturedly.

"And, now, for the cake…"

Joe reached for a knife and cut several slices, handing them out to everyone.

"This is all thanks to Gracie. It's her idea, and there's red velvet filling, which she knows is my favourite. Thank you, hen, for this. Especially the rolled icing sheep and lambing shed."

"Aye, it's so detailed!" Paul added. "It's braw! You should open your own shop."

"Aye, that's the plan," Grace said proudly.

"Wow," Paul replied, and held her gaze for a long moment, everyone including Joe could see the pride in his eyes. Another positive sign.

Suddenly, there was a frenzied barking and Rum and Whisky rushed over towards the cake. Rum had a ball in his mouth, and Whisky was giving chase, determined to get it back.

"Hey!" Joe called, laughing. He rose from his chair, making sure the dogs raced around the chair. The last thing anyone wanted was the cake getting knocked over. "Give over you two dafties!"

But the dogs, too excited and giddy, couldn't hear them, racing right and racing in a V around the table.

"Come here!" Annabelle called. "Joe, I dinnae want them knocking the table! There's glasses on here. They'll cut their paws!"

The dogs teared off, racing around the table, barking wildly.

Rum dived at Paul, landing squarely on his lap, and making the chair wobble.

"Look out!" Annabelle called as Paul's chair fell backwards, both him and dog in a heap on the dusty grass.

"Are you alright, Son?" Joe called in concern, but Paul was laughing, loving every second.

"Come on, let's play a proper game!" Paul cried, and stood up, brushing his clothes clean. He then took the tennis ball off Rum, kicking the tennis ball down the length of the field, and Rum and Whisky bounded after it.

"Och, well done, Son," Joe marvelled. "A grand idea. Are you alright?"

"Aye. Just a wee bump," Paul said amiably.

"Och, you've started something now..." Grace teased, and Paul shrugged amiably as Grace.

"It'll keep them happy for a wee while."

"You like dogs?" Joe asked. "Not all folk do. Especially sheep dogs. They can be a little bouncy and forward, a bit full on, aye?"

"Och, no, I love dogs," Paul said brightly. "I used to have a Westie when we were kids and our neighbour had a Border Terrier too."

Joe nodded, smiling, and Annabelle looked at him fondly.

"I'd love to get a pup one day. But I'd need to have a bit of land."

"Where are you living now?" Joe asked.

"I'm based in Aviemore. In the city centre. I work in I.T. but I'd swap that for farming any day. I love being outdoors, in the fresh air and all that."

"Aye? Even in the middle of winter? It's hard work in winter. The weather is unpredictable..."

"Aye, I dinnae doubt it," Paul said with admiration. "Especially with the kind of winters you get here, from what Grace has been telling me. Must be tough."

"Doesnae put you off?" Angus asked as he ate his cake but Paul shook his head.

"I'd love to do farming."

"Aye? Is that so?" Joe asked, interested as he finished his cake. He was liking him more and more now.

When the buffet was over, Robyn, Eilidh, Grace, Paul and Angus went off to dance.

"Are you no' joining us?" Robyn called but Joe shook his head.

"We're happy to watch you."

Robyn put some jazz on the portable CD player, and turned the volume up so that the music floated across the field.

Marianne and Maudie smiled at each other, and Enid nodded.

"That's another two sorted…" Enid announced.

Joe glanced across at Grace and smiled as she burst out laughing as Paul twirled her around, and they danced together.

Suddenly, the dogs came charging back across the field, Rum carrying the tennis ball, and charged straight for Paul and Grace.

"Woah!" Grace cried as Rum knocked her flying, and then they chased off across the field.

"Are you alright?" Paul asked, as he helped her up, brushing the dust off her shoulders.

"Aye, I'm fine," Grace laughed, and Paul put an arm around her shoulders. "Another drink?"

"Aye," Grace said. "That'd be nice…":

Paul and Grace walked over to the table and he poured her a glass of lemonade.

The chemistry between them was so electric that even Joe could see from here that they were going to end up a couple at some point.

It was only a question of when…

Chapter Twenty-five

 resent Day

After the photos, the party headed back to the house for the wedding breakfast. As everyone filed into the dining room, Grace checked her watch, and saw it wasn't long before they got the cake cutting part.

Making a discreet detour, Grace headed towards the kitchen to find Leanna piping the top tier of the cake.

"Och, Leanna that looks braw," Grace said, feeling her hopes rise, and she breathed a sigh of relief. The day would be saved.

"Have you had any luck with Archie? Has he spoken to the team?" Leanna asked.

"I havenae heard anything yet, but I'll try and find him, see if I can find the first cake. It's no' that you're no' doing a grand job. It's just that I put so much hard work into it."

"I know," Leanna said gently. "If it were me and I'd made my best friend's wedding cake, I'd want to find it too."

"Och, this is trickier than it looks!" Leanna laughed as she struggled to roll the icing.

"I can help," Grace said, wanting more than anything to share the burden, assuage her guilt for it going missing. "You're doing a grand job."

She rolled the icing into a tiny beehive and sheep, as she had done with the first cake.

"Grace, that's wonderful. I hope one day, I'll be a great as you."

"Och, it's nothing," Grace murmured. "I can teach you, if you like?"

"Really?"

"Aye, you could come and give me a hand in the bakery," Grace replied, dwelling on what Robyn had said at the hen night. "I could do with some help."

"Are you sure?" Leanna asked, eyes widening.

"Aye, of course."

"It's a deal."

They beamed at each other.

"Will it be ready in time for the cake cutting?"

"Aye, it will," Leanna said confidently, and Grace breathed a sigh of relief.

"Eilidh and Angus are gonnae love it. Thank you both so much. I should go and find Rhona, and Archie, come to think of it."

"Aye, of course. I'll get on with this," Leanna replied. "I think she was chatting to one of the guests outside."

"Aye?" Grace asked, with a light frown. "Who?"

"Let's just say your matchmaking plan seems to be working."

They both went to the door and looked out. Grace glanced up and down the corridor and did a double take to see Cedric and Rhona deep in conversation.

"How do they know each other?" Grace asked Leanna in surprise.

"Och, Cedric is a long-term pal of my grandad."

"They seem to be getting on well..." Grace said, with a smile.

"Aye. I think they'd make a braw match."

"I was thinking just the same thing..." Grace replied, make a mental note to go and find The Trinity and mention it.

Grace waited until Rhona and Cedric headed off towards the dining room and made to follow them when Mhairi came running out.

"Ma, can I take my cardigan off now?"

"Aye, sure, give it here, I'll take it upstairs. Go back to Da."

"Alright," Mhairi agreed, and handed over the cardigan. Grace watched her go, and then hurried upstairs.

~

The hallway was in shade as she hurried along, but then, she caught sight of a shadow moving under one closed doorway, which she vaguely remembered Rory said was his office, and hesitating at the doorway, she put a hand on the door handle, curiosity peaked. Everyone else, including Rory, was downstairs in the dining room.

She took a deep breath, and then let herself in. Rory's office was a bright, large room, painted in cream and lemon yellow, and the floor was carpeted. In the corner was a large mahogany desk, and a white bookcase filled with folders.

Next to the desk stood Archie, flipping through a ring binder.

"What are you doing in Rory's office?" Grace asked, frozen in the doorway.

"Oh, I was looking for a copy of the bill for the expenses for the wedding."

Archie glanced up nonchalantly, closing the binder and putting it back on the bookcase.

"Does he know you're in here? I thought you were busy today with the suppliers?"

"Yes, well I had a spare five minutes."

"But wouldn't he email you a document like that, instead of having it in a folder?"

Archie turned to her nonplussed.

"What are you doing here?"

"I saw a shadow in here and thought I'd investigate."

"Like a spy," Archie replied with thinly veiled sarcasm.

Grace bristled at his tone. "Have you had time to ask the team about the cake yet?"

"No. I haven't. How's your plan going to make another cake in time?" He checked his watch. "Not long to go now."

"Everything is going to plan. But I'd still like to find the other cake. It cannae have just vanished into thin air!"

"I think it would be best if you go with plan B and go with the other cake," Archie replied, putting the folder back on the bookcase and brushed past her. "Sorry I can't be of more help."

"I cannae believe it," Grace snapped. "Even after all this time, you havnae changed. You're letting me down at the last moment when I need your help the most. Again."

"Am I interrupting?"

Grace turned to see Paul standing right behind her.

"Excuse me," Archie said, and brushing past them, headed away down the corridor.

"Whit's all that about?" Paul asked, and Grace heard the tone in his voice. "Cannae stay away, can you? He's letting you down again? I could have told you that. After all, I've been the fool picking up after him, havenae I?"

"Paul, wait!" Grace cried, grabbing him arm and

pulling him inside the office and closing the door behind them. "It isnae what you think!"

"Aye? Well you could have fooled me. When Enid said you had to face your past, I dinnae think that's what she meant!"

Grace cut in before he could continue, her words coming out in a rush.

"I've lost the wedding cake, and Archie said he'd speak to the team to try and find it. Leanna is making another one to replace it, but after all the work I've done, I thought I have a right to see what Eilidh and Angus think of it!"

Paul's face fell, and he took a step forward with an exasperated sigh. "Why didnae you tell me?"

"I tried to tell you afore the wedding but you wouldnae listen!" Grace snapped back.

"But what are you doing in here?"

"I saw Archie in here and demanded what he was doing. He was looking through a binder. He claims it's for the expenses for today but when I questioned it, he changed the subject."

She turned to the bookcase, running her hand across the folders and took one out.

"Here it is. It's this one."

She opened it, and found on the second page, it was one of the expenses for the day. A printed email from Archie.

"Wait a moment," she murmured. "Take a look at this."

"What is it?"

"An invoice for the expenses for the catering, but the numbers dinnae match up. Archie is exhorting money from Rory."

"We need to tell Rory, The police-"

"That's no' all. The Landseer painting is missing."

"Do you think he's stolen it?" Paul asked, and Grace nodded.

"But how can we prove it?"

"This is half the proof," she said, waving the printout. "We just need to find the painting. But we need to get downstairs. We'll deal with this later."

The wedding breakfast was held in the drawing room which had now been set up with circular tables and was decorated with the same colour wedding favours as the chairs in the ceremony room. At the top table which stretched across the windows at the far side, Eilidh and Angus sat with Joe and Connie on either side, and Mhairi and Ollie, as well as Orion, who was Angus's best man.

Clink. clink. clink.

Everyone looked up to see Angus stand and clear his throat.

"Hullo, ladies and gentlemen," he said in his lilting, gentle voice, as he stood and tapped the glass. "Well, where to start? I'm to give a speech, which, I'll be honest is a wee bit unnerving."

He glanced at Eilidh shyly, and she beamed up at him. "As you all remember we met as bairns in the lambing shed when my father and Eilidh's grandfather introduced us. We all became good friends, and Eilidh joined our gang of three. Then, Eilidh and I grew up, she moved away and we stayed friends, until she returned to Mossbrae two years ago. She didnae realise I had feelings for her, and had for a long time. Slowly, we reconnected, and realised we felt more than friendship for each other... Helping her paint the cottage in the height of summer helped..."

Eilidh blushed and nodded, in between sips of champagne, as the rest of the congregation cheered.

"Tell us about the proposal!" Maudie called.

"I asked Eilidh to marry me last summer, at our home, Honeybee Cottage. I got the ring designed especially to look like honey on the comb and when I presented it to her, luckily, she said yes."

Eilidh nodded, her eyes filling with tears of happiness.

"I'd like to raise a toast," Angus said, raising his glass. "To my beautiful wife. Eilidh, I love you, and I always have. Thank you for becoming my wife."

"Thank you for becoming my husband," Eilidh whispered, smiling back at him as everyone raised their glass. "To Eilidh!"

Angus sat down and pulled her into a passionate, swoon worthy kiss.

"Och, it's so romantic," Maudie sighed, dabbing her eyes with a handkerchief as she turned to Nelly who nodded in agreement. They were seated together opposite the top table.

"Aye," Grace agreed, exchange a look with Robyn. "True love if ever we saw it."

They were interrupted by William laughing uproariously, the cutest baby laugh as Rory tickled his toes.

"Och, he's adorable! I miss the newborn stage sometimes..." Grace exclaimed, meeting Paul's gaze, and Robyn nodded in agreement, looking adoringly at the baby.

"Do you want another one of those?" Paul asked casually, gesturing towards William as he put an arm around her shoulders.

"What? Another baby?" she laughed, and then seeing the look on his face. "Are you being serious? With the bakery and the farm?"

"Aye, why not?" Paul asked, looking at her tenderly. "It might be fun. Do you remember the first time they tried to make us breakfast in bed?"

"Aye. The house stank of burnt toast for days!" Grace chuckled. "Mhairi was so proud of herself. She trampled cornflakes all over the kitchen floor..."

"Aye. That's right. Och, they were so small...I miss them being that wee..." Paul replied. "Are you not even tempted?"

He interlaced his fingers with hers and gave a warm smile.

"Och, I don't know..."

Robyn glanced down at her glass, adverting her gaze, thinking about the results of her test, and the temptation to tell everyone bubbled inside her. But the time wasn't right.

"Paul, the kids are at that stage when they are a bit more independent...And there's the bakery, and the farm, not to mention my age...Starting all over again, are you sure?"

"Och, a new baby would be wonderful!" Maudie exclaimed excitedly. "We havenae had a wean around at home since you had Mhairi. As for your age, it's no' too late, hen...I knew someone who had their last baby at forty-seven..."

"I think we're happy as we are..." Grace said with gentle firmness.

"You're right," Paul conceded, taking another sip of wine. "I'll just offer to babysit William whilst we're here."

"That should stem your baby fever," Grace said, smiling at him.

There was another *clink clink clink* of a fork on a glass and everyone turned to see Eilidh had rose from her chair.

"I just wanted to make a speech too. I wanted to make a toast to remember those we love who cannot be here today. Annabelle, and Marianne, we're thinking of you today, and we miss you so very much..."

She choked back tears as she raised her glass. "We

wish you were here today... To Annabelle and Marianne."

"To Annabelle and Marianne!"

Robyn and Grace exchanged a glance and seeing Grace's eyes welling up at the memory of their late mother.

Robyn reached over and gave her hand a squeeze. "Are you alright?"

"Aye. I am. I just miss Ma. She would have loved today."

"Aye, I know she would..."

Chapter Twenty-Six

he Past.

Autumn.

Cairnmhor Farm.

Grace checked the Aga and smiling, opened, filling the
kitchen with the scent of profiteroles as she pulled the
batch out and set it to cool on the side.

"What do you think?" she asked, turning to Robyn
who nodded, impressed.

"That's braw, Gracie. You're a brilliant baker. That
course is really helping, aye?"

"Aye, I suppose it is."

She glanced back at Robyn, feeling a sudden wave

of grief, and she burst into tears.

"It's alright," Robyn soothed her, putting her arms around her. "Ma's gonnae love it."

"Aye. I just cannae help thinking it'll be the last birthday with her..."

Robyn nodded, feeling the tears falling down her own cheeks.

"The doctor said we have until Christmas..." Robyn murmured.

The news that the cancer had spread was still fresh and raw, and Grace had come home on the first ferry she could. She had returned back to Cairnmhor to find Annabelle looking frail, having lost weight from the chemotherapy she had been receiving for the last three months. Grace could see she had already lost weight, highlighting her cheekbones and her dark eyes, and corn blonde hair. At fifty, she looked years younger, and Grace saw so much of her own, and Robyn's faces now, and wondered with churning dread how they were all going to cope with her passing when the time came. She, for one, was dreading it. She wanted, childishly, to freeze time, so that she wouldn't lose Annabelle.

"Aye, but Christmas is in three months time. I want this birthday to be the best birthday Ma has ever had. She's gonnae love it."

"She will. We'll make sure of it."

Grace turned and went into the living room where

Annabelle was resting on the sofa, wrapped in a tartan blanket.

"Ma?" She asked gently, and Annabelle opened her eyes, smiling at her.

"How is the croquembouche?" She asked. "I cannae wait to taste it."

"I need to assemble it, but it looks delicious."

They exchanged a smile, and Grace put her arms around her, hugging her gently.

"I love you, Ma."

"I love you, always," Annabelle murmured. "What time is everyone arriving?"

"This afternoon. I need to prepare the buffet food."

"Do you need any help?" Annabelle asked but Grace shook her head.

"Robyn is helping me. Da and Angus are on their way back."

They looked out of the window now at the rainy September day, to where the quad bike was coming along the path with Joe and Angus, followed by the dogs. They had been out on the hill checking the ewes ahead of the breeding season.

Annabelle smiled softly. "I'll go and get the kettle on and make us a brew."

"That would be lovely."

"Och, It's stoating down out there!" Angus exclaimed, as he came in, removing his boots and coat. "Rum, dinnae shake all over the carpet!"

Rum barked happily, and wandered into the living room to greet Annabelle.

"Something smells braw!" Joe said cheerfully. "Is that the cake I can smell?"

Grace nodded. "Hands off, though. I need to ice it."

"I love chocolate orange," Joe said, as he went into the living room to greet Annabelle.

"Are you alright?" Angus asked, seeing Grace's face, and she shook her head.

"No," she murmured, and Angus put an arm around her.

"It'll be alright," he said, and Grace was almost convinced.

That afternoon, Annabelle's favourite jazz tunes were playing on the CD player in the corner of the living room, and between them, Robyn, Grace and Angus had made a delicious buffet between them. Grace had made roast chicken thighs with lemon and paprika.

"These are braw!" Angus exclaimed as he tucked into one. "You should make these your signature dish."

"Aye? Beats beans on toast!" Grace replied. It was her second attempt at making them, and she was pleased with the results if she didn't say so herself.

The doorbell rang, and Grace, went to answer it, licking the caramel sauce from her fingers. The Trinity, Marianne and Eilidh had arrived with arms full of presents for Annabelle. They bustled in and greeted her brightly, and went into the living room to greet Annabelle, who was sitting on the sofa, finishing her tea.

"Happy birthday!" Maudie and Nelly called, handing over the presents.

"Och, you're looking braw, hen," said Enid, sitting next to Annabelle on the sofa whilst Nelly and Maudie handed her the presents.

"Thank you," Annabelle said, summoning a smile, as Marianne kissed her cheek in greeting.

"I brought some honey cakes too," Eilidh said, offering the box to Grace in the kitchen. "I made them myself, so fingers crossed they're nice."

"Thanks," Grace replied. "They'll be braw. We'll have them for pudding."

"Do you need a hand?" Eilidh asked, tucking her hands into the pockets of her jeans to hide her natural shyness.

"No, it's alright," Grace replied, assuming the mother role and gesturing to the dining chair. "Sit yourself down and grab a plate."

"Thanks," Eilidh said, tucking a strand of hair behind her ear as she helped herself to the chicken thighs.

"How's university?" Angus asked, sitting opposite her.

"It's braw. I'm having a grand time," Eilidh replied and as she smiled, her whole face lit up.

"Met anyone special?" Grace asked casually as she glanced between Angus and Eilidh. Honestly, the sparks between them were lighting up the kitchen.

"Oh, no. I've been too busy," Eilidh said, with a mouthful of chicken thigh.

"Och! These are braw! did you make them yourself?"

"Aye. It's just the second time doing it."

"I said she should make them her signature dish," Angus added.

"Aye!" Echoed the Trinity. "Well done, Gracie!"

"We ought to get the candles for the croquembouche," Grace added, scraping the chair back and heading to the pantry and brought out the croquembouche.

"Jings!" Robyn exclaimed. "Grace, that's amazing!"

"Thanks," Grace replied as she laid it out on the table, admiring the great tower of profiteroles covered in caramel sauce. "I made it last week for the first time and I've been practicing this weekend."

Joe walked into the kitchen, and they looked up to see he had tears in his eyes.

"Och, Gracie…" he said, with a sniff. Grace felt her own eyes fill with tears. He was not a man to show his emotions very often, so the fact he had been brought to tears, meant it really meant a lot to him. "Your Ma's gonnae love this."

"Let me see!" Annabelle called, like a small child, and Enid and Maudie helped her to her feet, and lead her into the kitchen, and Grace watched as Annabelle's face lit up with delight at the sight of the croquembouche, and she clapped her hands over her mouth in delight.

"Och, Grace, that's the best birthday cake I've ever had."

"Happy birthday," Grace said, as she added a couple of candles and lit them.

Everyone gathered around and began to sing Happy Birthday, but all Grace was watching as she sang, was her mother's face, and lifted her phone taking several photos, wanting to hold this memory forever.

Chapter Twenty-Seven

 resent Day

"That was absolutely delicious," Grace said as she laid her knife and fork on her empty plate and let out a satisfied sigh. With melon for starters, roast beef and all the trimmings for main, and for pudding, the most delicious honey and whisky ice cream and fresh raspberries.

Maudie nodded in agreement.

"Absolutely braw."

"I see Odette doesnae seem to have enjoyed it quite so much."

She watched now as the older woman stood, brushing crumbs from her outfit and hurried out of the room.

Grace had a sudden urge to follow her, remembering the missing painting.

"Maudie, would you excuse me," she murmured.

"Och, of course, hen. Got some investigating to do?"

Grace did a double take, looking at her, wondering if she knew.

"Aye," she smiled. "Something like that."

Checking no-one else was around, she followed Odette, watching her slip through the kitchens. Grace felt her heart hammering, remembering the cake and hoping Odette wasn't the one who had taken the cake. She couldn't think of a reason why…

She followed her out to the where the bins were and caught sight of Odette struggling to lift something. With her back to her Grace couldn't see it, but she rushed forward.

"Odette, wait!"

Odette spun around and dropped the painting.

"What are you doing?" Grace asked softly, so as not to antagonise her.

"What does it look like?!" Odette hollered. "That wee bitch is responsible for it!"

She gestured to the painting. "And he knew all along!"

Grace turned to see Rory standing in the doorway.

"Aye, Odette, that's true," Rory replied, folding his arms. "But I only moved the painting, I didnae want to cause further trouble."

"You've done enough!" Odette spat, throwing the painting to the ground before storming out. "I'm leaving!"

Grace sighed with relief as she watched her go. "At least she didnae damage the painting."

Rory nodded. "I'll put it back up as soon as the wedding is done."

"I need to talk to you," Grace replied. "I found Archie in your office earlier. He had these."

She handed the papers to him, and he read them, his face clouding.

"I shall speak to him."

"No, I'll do it," Grace replied. "I lost the cake earlier and I cannae find it…"

There was a clatter, and she glanced at the bins, then spotted the cake boxes which had contained her cake.

"I think we found the cake," Rory replied, shaking his head. "I'm so sorry, Grace."

She let out an exasperated sigh, then spotted cake covered footprints on the floor. They belonged to a man's shoes, one Grace would recognise instantly.

"Something tells me he has something to do with it…"

"I'll speak to him," Rory said but Grace shook her head.

"I'll do it."

It was time to face her past.

She headed out to the front entrance and spotted him closing the car boot.

"Grace," he said, not meeting her eye.

"I found the cake boxes. In the bins. And your shoe prints beside them."

She glanced down at his now freshly cleaned shoes. "Why did destroy them?"

Closing the car door, he turned to face her.

"Want to keep it down?" He hissed. "Like you've said, it's your friend's wedding. You didnae want to ruin it."

"All I want to know is why?" She demanded. "To get back at me?"

Archie blew out an exasperated breath, his gaze levelling with hers.

"Honestly Grace, you're full of yourself."

"I'm right though, aye?" Grace shot back, letting out a mirthless laugh as she held his gaze, shaking her head in disappointment. "You still want revenge on me, even after all these years. I canna believe it."

"Can you blame me?" Archie asked, shaking his head. "All you were bothered about was your family and Paul."

"Paul was a kind, supportive friend. Unlike you, no' caring for anyone but yourself," she shot back, her voice breaking. "Where were you when my mother was dying?"

Chapter Twenty-Eight

he Past.

The call Grace had been dreading came as soon as she had got home after an exhausting twelve hour shift.

"Hen," Joe said gently as she took the call. "It's time to come home. She's been asking for you."

"I'll be right there," she replied without hesitation.

Surprisingly, Archie had offered her a lift, but now, as she looked out of the living room window for car head-lights, she felt a wave of panic. It was already half past five, and she had to catch the six pm ferry.

There was a beep of car horn and she almost sobbed with relief.

"There you are!" she cried in relief as Archie let himself in. "I'm ready to go."

Archie frowned at her. "Go where?"

"You said you were gonnae give me a lift to the ferry," Grace replied, trying not to panic.

"Ah," Archie sighed. "Look, I'm knackered. You'll have to get a taxi."

"A taxi?" Grace cried. "But I need to get home. They need me."

But Archie wasn't listening. He went into the kitchen and got a beer out of the fridge.

"Fine," Grace replied, and reached for her mobile, and dialled a number.

It seemed an age as she waited, but then, she heard the beep of a car horn, and almost sobbing with relief, tugged the door open.

"Is that your knight in shining armour?" Archie asked sarcastically as she tugged her case outside.

"Yes," Grace said with thinly veiled sarcasm. "It is. I'll collect my things when I come back."

"What?" Archie demanded.

"You heard me. It's over."

With that, she dragged the case to the awaiting car.

"Thank you so much Paul," she said through the passenger window.

"That's no problem," he replied, and she got in, feeling a weight lifting from her shoulders.

Hours later, the harbour of Mossbrae came into view, and Grace felt overwhelmed at the sight of the promenade with the beach below, and The Dog and Duck, the church and a row of houses, including the old Mackay sweet shop opposite the harbour. The air smelt of peat, salt and home, and Grace felt the tears spring to her eyes as the ferry came to a halt and everyone began to depart.

Pulling her small wheelie case with her, Grace walked down the ramp, looking for Angus, who was waiting next to the Land Rover at the top of the promenade.

"Hullo," Angus greeted her as she reached him, and she could see the tiredness etched on his face, and she felt her heart hammering with dread.

"Am I too late?"

"No," he replied shaking his head, and she flung herself into his arms, sobbing quietly.

Angus shushed her, stroking her hair. "It's alright, Gracie. Let's get home."

They set off, heading away from the harbour, watching slowly as the village became rolling fields and conifer forests, and Cairnmhor Farm came into view as the early morning sunlight shone down across the valley. Grace watched the hills roll past, hoping this wouldn't be the last morning she would share with Annabelle.

. . .

She felt a sudden pang of fear that she would be too late, picturing her mother now, her corn blonde hair, blue eyes, high cheekbones, soft, gentle face, and her mind went back to that birthday before they found out the cancer had spread. She thought about Annabelle putting her arms around her, and holding her. Grace clung onto that memory as they turned right and drove up onto the gravelled driveway.

"We're here," Angus murmured as Grace turned and saw Cairnmhor Farm come into view, the whitewashed farmhouse looked as it always had done, with the paddocks flanking either side, and the rest of the hill farm leading out up the hillside at the back.

They parked the car and got out, Grace tugging her case from the boot.

"Hello, hen!" Joe called from the open door, and Grace rushed into his arms, and he held her for a long time.

"It's good to see you. I'm so glad you're home."

She heard his voice gruff with emotion, and she could hear that he had been crying.

"I'm glad too," Grace replied as she stepped into the familiar kitchen. It was warm, cosy and smelt faintly of rosemary and garlic, just as it had done when they were kids.

. . .

The dogs came to her, young Dram, and an aging Betty, whining with concern and wagging their tails solemnly, as though they knew something was amiss. Grace petted them fondly, and they didn't rush, barking with feral abandon as they usually did. They licked her gently, and pressed wet noses into her hand, which made Grace want to cry more. It was as though they knew, she marvelled, just like Eilidh said bees knew when someone was about to leave.

"Come through," Joe urged her and she followed him into the living room. The living room looked so different from when she was here last. Since Annabelle's time had grown closer, Joe had asked if she was able to be at home, and not in a hospice. The doctor had agreed, and Annabelle had come home four weeks ago, where she planned to spend her last days. Between them, Joe and Angus had converted the living room into a bedroom for Annabelle who was finding it difficult to get up and down the stairs, and Marianne had been coming daily as well as a nurse, to come and take care of her. Annabelle had been grateful, pleased that she could spend her final days admiring the views and have some peace in familiar surroundings.

"Hello, Ma," Grace greeted her gently, sitting down besides her. Annabelle was laying in the sofa bed, wrapped in a tartan duvet cover, head resting on two comfy pillows.

Annabelle murmured something she couldn't quite

hear, and Grace leant forward to listen, hoping she would repeat it, but she didn't.

"Ma? I love you," Grace murmured but Annabelle didn't reply. "Ma?"

For a moment, Grace felt a surge of panic that she was too late.

"It's alright," Joe said, sitting in the armchair opposite. "She can hear you. She's gone to sleep, hen."

But in her heart, Grace could see this wasn't entirely true, given how shallow Annabelle's breathing was now. She knew the time was close.

"I love you, Ma," she said gently. "I'm here. We're all here."

Annabelle gave a barely audible sound, and Grace looked relieved, and slipped her hand into her mother's. It felt cool, and soft, just as she remembered when she was little when Annabelle used to flour her hands before baking.

"I'm here, Ma," Grace murmured. "It's a wonderful sunny day today, not a cloud in the sky…" Grace went on, trying to fill the silence should she burst into tears.

"I'll make us a brew," Angus said, and went into the kitchen.

"Where's Robyn?"

"I'm here," Robyn called back. "Is it warm enough in here?"

"Aye, it's grand, lass," Joe assured her.

"How was the ferry over?" Robyn asked Grace as she sat next to her now, taking Annabelle's other hand.

"It was a good crossing."

"Aye, same here. Ma sleeps a lot nowadays. It's the morphine. We were told to give it her for the pain, but it makes her tired…"

Grace nodded. "So she's no' in pain?"

"No, not at all," Robyn reassured her, her voice almost a whisper.

She turned to Annabelle now and saw for herself her breathing was getting more shallow.

"We're all here, Ma," Grace repeated. "Me, Da, Robyn and Angus."

"Aye, that's right, Ma," Angus agreed.

For a moment, Grace met his eyes, and her heart broke to see that they had both been crying and her heart broke, knowing it was the end.

"We love you so, so much."

Annabelle squeezed Grace's hand, and Grace smiled sadly back, sniffing quietly.

She glanced over at Robyn, who was wiping her eyes now, trying not to make too much noise as she cried silently.

"It's alright, Ma," Grace murmured. "We're all here…"

Annabelle raised her hand and stroked Grace's cheek, a faint smile spreading across her face, and then, her hand slid down to the covers, and Grace felt it go slack in hers, and she felt the tears falling, unbidden, down her cheeks.

"Och, Ma," Grace sobbed, kissing her mother's forehead, and cradled her face, not willing to let her go just yet, her heart breaking. Then she turned to Robyn, who pulled her into her arms, holding her. Joe and Angus moved to her, pulling her into a group hug, united in grief.

~

Three Weeks Later.

"So, what do you think of Paul?" Robyn asked Grace, a lightly mischievous tone in her voice. Robyn, who had stayed resolutely single whilst she was at university, determined to concentrate on her studies, was determined to matchmake anyone else she could think of.

"He's wonderful," Grace replied without hesitation, knowing exactly where Robyn was going with this. "He's kind, thoughtful, he's one of my best friends."

She couldn't help but picture his face now, the kind blue eyes, aquiline features, and tousled red hair which she secretly found so attractive.

"Friend? Just a friend?" Robyn asked. "You dinnae fancy him even a little bit?"

"Och, It's hardly the right time, aye? I'm no' ready for another relationship."

"You need someone else to comfort you. You cannae be strong for everyone and ignore yourself," Robyn replied sagely.

"I dinnae want to hurt Paul. He's wonderful and we get on really well."

"So why not have a date and see how it goes?"

Robyn asked, laying back on the bed. "So, what do you say? Ask him out."

"I cannae do that," Grace replied, shaking her head.

"He fancies you rotten..." Robyn added

"He's really nice, aye."

"Sounds like you like him back," Eilidh added, sipping her own drink. "Anyone fancy another drink?"

Grace shook her head. "I just prefer to matchmake other people."

"Och! Now you sound like The Trinity! Whom do you have in mind?" Angus chuckled.

"Och, isnae it obvious?" Grace grinned as Eilidh got up to get another drink. "You and Eilidh of course!"

"Me and Eilidh?" Angus laughed, with a light frown, glancing back at the open doorway. "Eilidh has a boyfriend, and she's happy. I'm too much of a good friend to destroy that."

"But you're dotty about her!" Grace cried.

"Och! Behave!" Angus laughed. "Och, aye, I forgot, you're practically planning our wedding!"

"Dinnae give me ideas!" Grace chuckled.

"Och, you're incorrigible. Eilidh and I.. it's complicated."

"No," Robyn said, smiling pointedly at him. "She's your future wife."

Then she and Grace looked at each other and burst out laughing.

"Alright," Grace conceded when they calmed down. "If it will keep you from matchmaking and plotting, and scheming, then I'll do it."

"Ma liked him, you know," Robyn had added. "Think on it…"

The ceremony began as everyone listened to the lone piper outside St Anthony's church on that mild morning, and Grace felt her throat thicken with emotion, making a silent prayer that she was going to get through today.

"I'm sorry I'm late," said a voice, and she felt a warm hand gently take hers. She turned and saw Paul standing there, wearing a navy suit which picked out his blue eyes and his red-gold hair.

"Hello," she croaked.

"Hello. I came to pay my respects."

"Och, Paul, thank you for coming, it's so good to see you!" she said, her voice breaking as she flung her arms around his neck. Her heart gave a little surge of gratitude, and as he held her tightly, she knew she could get through this.

It was a simple ceremony, with a piper, and several of Annabelle's favourite jazz songs as opposed to hymns, and Grace even heard herself humming along. The church was filled with all of her friends and family, and Grace felt overwhelmed at how many people had come to pay their respects. Annabelle had been well loved, she thought, reminding her of what a wonderful woman her mother had been.

. . .

The wake was held at Cairnmhor Farm, and Grace had made a small buffet. There was a grand selection of ham lattice, pork pies, freshly made sausage rolls, and smoked salmon amuse bouche, as well as smoked salmon quiche, vegetable quiche, and mini venison pies. But despite the delicious array of food, Grace didn't feel hungry.

Suddenly, a wave of grief hit her, and tears spilled down her cheeks as she tried to keep her composure.

Robyn put her arm around her, as tears sprang to her eyes. "It's alright. It'll be alright…" she murmured as Grace stifled a sob.

"Come on, lass," Paul murmured, and put his arm around her. "It'll be alright…I'm here for you."

He put his arm around her, and even in her grief, and Grace felt safe, and secure, knowing he meant it.

Chapter Twenty-Nine

resent Day

Archie looked back at her with a cold stare but she saw a twitch of emotion in his eyes.

"Nowhere! That's where you were!" Grace shot back. "You were too busy fooling around with Clara. You've never thought of me."

"I do regret that," Archie admitted, his face softening. "I'm sorry for the way I treated you. I thought you were delayed in finding the cake you'd need me."

"So you thought you'd ruin my best friend's day? To try and win me back? You've got a twisted way with things! I suppose you're showing what a good friend you are to Rory, eh? Stealing his money."

Archie paled.

"I found the papers. You think you're so clever, trying to pull the wool over everyone's eyes…"

"You say anything," Archie said, taking a step forward, his face crumbling into a snarl. "And you'll regret it. You think you're so fancy, with your Instagram page, and your article for Visit Scotland. That's always been your problem, you think you're better than everyone else, even when you grew up on a bloody farm!"

He stepped menacingly, and Grace was relieved to hear the wail of police sirens, and saw Rory and Paul making their way towards them.

"I can explain!" Archie cried as the police handcuffed him.

"Aye, I hope you can. Now, be sure to tell them the whole truth," Rory replied, watching them go, as Paul walked over to her and took her in his arms.

"It's alright," he murmured. "I'm here."

And she immediately felt like coming home.

The reception was in full swing as they walked back inside.

Rory took the microphone and cleared his throat, indicating the live ceilidh band. "Ladies and gentlemen. Let's get this party started!"

There was a resounding cheer and everyone pushed their chairs back, clearing the floor for dancing and partying.

"I cannae get stuck into the cake!" Maudie announced.

"Och! We havenae cut the cake!" Eilidh cried, and then, looked around the room with a light frown. "Wait, where is the cake?"

At that moment, the dining room door opened and Leanna and Rhona came in with the wedding cake on a black hostess trolley.

"Here it is!" Eilidh cried, and Grace felt dizzy with relief at the sight of it.

The cake was almost better than the original, a triple-layered cream and lemon yellow, with the rolled icing figurines on the top layer.

"That's so beautiful!" Eilidh cried in delight above the sea of applause and cheering.

Grace felt her heart hammering, knowing her time was up. Could she get away with not saying anything?

"Where's Gracie?" Eilidh was calling, and she felt her gaze on her like a spotlight.

"Gracie, come here!"

"It'll be alright," Paul murmured in her ear, squeezing her hand reassuringly. "No-one will care."

"I will care, though," Grace murmured as she allowed Eilidh to catch her.

"Come here!" Eilidh cried, flinging her arms around her. "This cake is the best one I've ever seen. Thank you so much! You're a genius!"

Seeing tears in her eyes, Grace knew she couldn't continue with this charade, knowing what had happened with the original cake. How could she keep lying to her best friend?

Not knowing what to do, feeling torn and utterly helpless, she burst into tears.

"Och, Gracie!" Eilidh laughed, clutching her tightly. "It's alright!"

"No, it isnae!" Grace sobbed, and with some force, pulled Eilidh away, and turned from her. "Excuse me, I need some fresh air!"

She hurried towards the open patio doors and the freedom of the terrace.

"What's going on?" Angus asked in concern, as everyone turned to look.

"It's made her all a bit emotional," Robyn chipped in.

"Aye," Paul agreed. "I'll go after her."

"I'll go."

Eilidh gently brushed past everyone and followed Grace out to the bench.

"Are you alright, hen?" She asked, sitting next to her.

"No," Grace sobbed. "I'm sorry. I'm ruining your wedding day, after I promised I would give you the best day ever."

"No, dinnae fret!" Eilidh cried grabbing her hand. "I dinnae know what you're talking about."

"The cake isnae the one I made. I lost the cake."

"What are you talking about?" Eilidh asked, and she gave a ragged sigh.

"I lost the cake. Rhona and Leanna have made a new

one, and I put the figurines on the top so that you wouldnae worry."

"Gracie," Eilidh cried, throwing her arms around her. "I dinnae mean to hurt your feelings by saying this, but I dinnae care about the cake."

Grace looked up at her. "What?"

"I'm more bothered that you're here to celebrate with me. you're my best friend, and now, my sister-in-law. I wouldnae be here if it wasn't for you."

"I wanted to give you the perfect day."

"But you have," she replied. "I adore you."

Grace gave a sniff, trying to calm herself and Eilidh pulled her to her, hugging her tighter.

"Come on," she said as she pulled aye. "Come and watch us do our first dance. I think you'll like it."

"Is everything alright?" Angus asked as he came out onto the terrace. "Gracie? Eilidh?"

"Everything is fine," Eilidh replied, put an arm around Grace's shoulders.

"Come here," Angus said, putting his arms around her too. "It's a difficult day for me too. I understand."

"Me too," Robyn added, her own voice cracking, and she joined them in a group hug.

"Dinnae forget me," Joe said, and Grace smiled as he joined them. "Sometimes, we have to face our past in order to face our future," Joe said, echoing Enid's words.

"Aye," Grace agreed. "I know."

"Shall we go and have a dance?" Eilidh suggested, and together, they went back into the dining room.

"Come cut the cake first!" Angus laughed, and Eilidh rushed back over, cutting it to cheers and rounds of applause.

∼

"Before our first dance, I want to make a toast," Angus said, turning his gaze Grace. "I wanted to thank my big sister. She's gone out of her way to make this day perfect, and if it weren't for her love of match-making, we wouldnae have a wedding today. Thank you for being the glue that kept us together when we lost Ma, even though you were grieving too. You're the best big sister that a brother could ask for. You're kind, thoughtful and always put others first. Well, tonight, I want you to put yourself first, and enjoy yourself, and have fun. I'll see you on the dance floor!"

There were resounding cheers as everyone hugged Grace, who wiped away a tear, especially when Mhairi and Ollie rushed over to hug her.

The ceilidh band struck up a beautiful version of The Most Beautiful Girl in The World.

"Remember this one?" Eilidh grinned. "We danced to this at your wedding."

"Aye," Grace said, wiping away happy tears. "I remember."

Paul put an arm around her, pulling her close as

Angus took Eilidh's hand and lead her onto the dance floor.

"I love you," he murmured into her hair, and she glanced up at him, eyes shining.

"I love you too."

"I couldnae think of a better day," Eilidh said, as Angus twirled her around. "But my feet are killing me."

"Take your shoes off," Angus said easily and she burst out laughing.

"Och! You cannae take your shoes off whilst dancing to Prince!" She cried, aghast. "Especially at a wedding!"

"Och, Paddington, it's your wedding. You can do just what you want!" He gave a soft chuckle.

"Aye, you're right," she replied, slipping her shoes off, and Angus grinned at her as they continued to dance.

There was another round of applause as the song ended, and Paul turned to Grace.

"May I have this dance?"

She smiled and took his hand as he led her to the dance floor as the band struck up a traditional jig, and as they did, she remembered the night they had their first date, all those years ago…

Chapter Thirty

he Past.

Aviemore.

That evening, Paul met Grace after work, and they went for dinner to The Runaway Haggis again.

Tonight, like every Friday night, was a theme night, and tonight was an Italian theme and Grace and Paul were looking forward to it. Especially when Grace had checked the menu online and saw that there was orange tiramisu for desert.

"I love a theme night!" Grace announced as they walked through the door.

"Aye, I cannae wait to get to desert," Paul replied, as he followed her in, and they were lead to their table, a quiet booth in a corner of the restaurant, overlooking the kitchens.

"Really?" Grace asked, with a mischievous grin.

"Och, no!" Paul cried, blushing. "I didnae mean it like that. I meant the desert. The tiramisu…"

Grace couldn't help but smile.

"Me neither."

Paul shrugged off his coat and Grace was surprised to see he was wearing a suit, and her gaze took him in.

"You look really good," Grace said, looking up at him, and Paul grinned at her.

"Aye? You think?"

"You look good in a suit."

"Thanks," Paul said as she shrugged off her own coat off to reveal a dark emerald sequinned dress. It was her favourite dress, one she had had for a long time but had been waiting for an opportunity to wear it.

She turned to see Paul's gaze squarely on her. He looked as her in amazement, as though she was the most beautiful thing he had ever seen, Grace in turn felt a crackle of something between them, and she knew this date was different from any other date she would go on from now on.

"You look wonderful. Green really suits you."

"Thank you," Grace replied, smiling. "Shall we order?"

Paul nodded, unable to tear his gaze away from her.

"Paul, you're staring…"

Flushing, he cleared his throat, and pointed to the menu. They glanced up to see the waitress making her way over. Paul ordered two calamari starters, two pizzas for main, and orange tiramisu for pudding, as well as a bottle of white to share.

. . .

The wine arrived and Paul poured them both a glass.

"Here's to us," Paul announced, raising his glass.

"To us," Grace agreed, touching her glass against his.

Paul took a long sip of his wine and put the glass down.

"Paul, wait... I have to confess I feel a bit nervous."

He met her gaze, chuckling in surprise, and Grace felt a flutter in the pit of her stomach. "Why?"

"Well, we're on a proper first date."

"Aye, we are," Paul agreed. "I'm a bit nervous too, but dinnae fret. We're gonnae have a good time."

Grace nodded and felt reassured when he placed his hand on hers.

"Thank you for being so supportive these last few months," Grace said, looking up at him. "I want you to know I'm really grateful."

"Och, it's nothing. We've been friends for such a long time," Paul replied, looking into her eyes and Grace felt her heart race as he did so, and the spark of attraction between them flared. She suddenly didn't want to leave this restaurant.

She wanted to sit here forever, with Paul.

"I hope, whatever happens, we'll always be friends," she said. "If we take the plunge with this romance and by some bad luck, it doesnae work out, we'll be friends."

"Aye," Paul agreed. "You'll always have me as a friend, Gracie, I'm always here for you. Now, shall we order?"

Grace nodded. "I cannae wait to try that orange tiramisu."

"The best tiramisu I had was in Rome."

"Have you ever been to Italy?" Grace asked.

"Aye. Only for the summer though. I lived in a little apartment near the Colosseum last year. It was brilliant."

"I'd love to go to Rome," Grace replied, liking him even more. "I love the history."

"Aye, it's a very historical city," Paul replied, as he perused the menu. "There's so much to visit and see whilst you're there. There's the writer's museum in the centre, near the Spanish Steps. Percy Shelley lived there for a while."

"Oh? I love Percy Shelley."

"He's buried in the Protestant cemetery in the centre of Rome, it's near Ottaviano, and there's a pyramid in the cemetery."

"A pyramid?" Grace asked, not knowing whether to laugh or not.

"Aye. A proper one."

Grace shook her head in surprise.

"We should go to Rome one day," Paul said as the waitress came to the table to take their order.

· · ·

The pizzas arrived, and they were delicious, with gooey stringy mozzarella and rich, herby tomato sauce. The ham and pineapple topping was sweet, rich, and made it the best pizza Grace had eaten for a long time.

"You have a bit of cheese..." Paul said, wiping her chin with his thumb and making her blush.

"Thanks," Grace replied, with a giggle. It felt good to laugh again, with losing Annabelle, it felt like she hadn't laughed in such a long time...

"This is what I'd love to do," Paul said as he finished his pizza. "Run a farm, and then, on warm summer evenings sit outside on the patio with the pizza oven, and eat home made pizzas and admire the view. What do you think?"

"That sounds wonderful."

"Maybe you could enjoy it with me," Paul smiled at her.

"Aye, maybe I could," Grace replied, and she began to wonder if he could be right. She had a vision of them together at Cairnmhor, enjoying the pizza, admiring the view, and had a very clear sense he would fit right in, shearing the sheep alongside Angus and Joe.

She smiled across at him.

He had potential for sure.

The tiramisus arrived and both they tucked in with barely concealed glee.

"Orange tiramisu," Grace announced as she took a mouth watering bite, resisting the desire to lick her spoon clean-that could be misinterpreted on so many levels- "is the best pudding I have ever tasted!"

"I told you it was wonderful," Paul replied with a warm smile. "I mean, how can anyone not enjoy tiramisu?"

"I know," Grace replied. "It's the best pudding you could ever have."

"It's my favourite too," Paul said, and Grace knew, deep in herself, that he was the one for her.

Reaching forward, she took hold of his hand, his grip warm and soft in hers, and she smiled at him.

After the meal, Grace and Paul walked back to the car, hand in hand, heading back to Paul's car.

"No' bad for a first proper date, aye?"

"Aye," Paul asked, as he walked alongside her, and then, her heart sang as he slipped his hand into hers. "We should do this again some time."

"Aye. I'll have to get the tiramisu recipe," Grace said. "I need to cook it for you."

"You're gonnae cook for me?" Paul asked, glancing at her in surprise and she nodded, wanting suddenly to impress him, for him to see her potential as a good chef, and she realised, girlfriend. He was one of the nicest men she had ever met, he was kind and sweet, and best of all, a best friend. That was the best foundation, Annabelle had told her, a solid friendship from which you could build on. Grace knew in her heart that this was something more.

"Grace," Paul's voice broke into her thoughts and she glanced at him now in the quiet street, bathed in the light of the street lights like some Christmas romantic comedy.

"Aye?" She asked, turning to him, feeling his grip on her hand, so comforting and protective.

"I wanted to say, I really like you."

"I like you too," Grace said, smiling at him.

"No, I really do like you. As more than a friend."

He took a step towards her, and for a moment, she thought he was going to kiss her. But then, he took her hand and placed it on his chest, so she could feel his heart beat. His heart was racing.

"This is how I feel whenever I'm around you," he said. "I cannae stop thinking about you, and the thought I'm gonnae see you again makes my heart want to burst with happiness."

Grace took a step closer, looking up into his blue eyes. "I feel the same about you."

He looked delighted, and then, she reached up and kissed him. it was a soft, dry kiss, but with the promise of so much more lingering under the surface.

Grace pulled away and Paul looked dumbfounded, as though waking from a dream, then he pulled her back to him and kissed her passionately, and Grace was hit with a wave of longing for him. It started in her toes, making its way up her whole body, and in response she threw her arms around his neck and clung to him, kissing him back for all she was worth.

They pulled apart, and Paul regarded her with such longing, she knew that tonight was the night when their friendship changed forever into something much more wonderful.

Paul pulled back, looking at her with pure joy.

"I've wanted to kiss you for so long. I cannae quite believe it that you've kissed me."

"I've wanted to kiss you for a while now," Grace admitted, and then pulled him back to her, kissing him again. It was a deeper kiss, more passionate than the first, and she knew in that instant, Robyn and Annabelle had been right.

He was the right one for her.

"Let's go home," Paul said, and flagged down a taxi, and they got inside, giggling like teenagers.

Chapter Thirty-One

 resent Day.

Paul's voice broke into her thoughts.

"Are you alright?"

"Aye, I'm fine," Grace replied, glancing at him. "I was thinking back to the night we got engaged."

"Aye? I remember being so nervous, but I'm so glad you said yes."

Paul reached for her hand and squeezed it tightly.

She glanced back, her heart racing at the sight of him, her heart race at the sight of him in his dark grey suit, his dark red hair brushing the collar of his cream shirt. He really had been the one for her. Robyn had been right all along.

"It's been a braw wedding, hasnae it?" Grace asked, glancing over at Robyn and Orion now, who were dancing together.

"Aye, I think it's definitely set the bar," Paul agreed. "Although, dinnae tell Eilidh I said this, but, personally, I still think our wedding was the best."

Grace nodded. "It was the best day of my life."

Then she pulled him to her and kissed him deeply, passionately.

The song came to an end and then, and another lively jig struck up which was met with resounding cheers. Paul and Grace left the dance floor arm in arm, to make the most of the buffet. It was a delicious spread, Grace thought as she admired the array of food on the table, and helped herself to a plate.

"They're having a wonderful time, aren't they?" Paul said, admiring Mhairi and Ollie now as they danced with Nelly and Maudie, Eilidh, Angus and Joe.

"Aye, they love a good wedding. And I have to say, we do grand weddings!" Grace replied, fondly.

"Aye, I cannae disagree with you there."

"Da! Come back and dance!" Ollie called, and Mhairi beckoned,.

"Go on," Grace grinned, and Paul went to join them, and Grace watched them, feeling a surge of happiness. She tucked into a slice of ham lattice and spotting Robyn with another full plate of buffet food.

"All that dancing giving you an appetite, Robyn, aye?"

"Aye, something like that! Want some?" Robyn asked, her mouth full as she offered her the plate of food. "This smoked salmon quiche is almost as good as yours!"

"I'll have to get recipe," Grace replied with a grin. Then, she put her arm around Robyn's shoulders as they watched Eilidh and Angus dance. "I have to say, we set the bar for weddings don't we?"

"Aye, we do," Robyn grinned. "It reminds me of the night you and Paul got engaged."

Grace nodded, remembering it fondly. "He was so nervous! We went for a walk in the formal rose gardens, and he was sweating! Then, he got down on one knee and proposed, and I knew instantly, that I was would say yes."

"Once you've met the One for you, you know," Robyn agreed.

"Aye, and all it took was a wee push in the right direction," Maudie added, behind them. "I think we're quite good at the whole matchmaking thing, wouldn't you agree?"

"We're the best!" Robyn grinned.

"Och, I dinnae think I've ever seen anything so romantic!" Maudie said, dabbing her eyes with a hand-kerchief as she turned her attention to watch Angus and Eilidh dance, and Grace smiled at her. "This is a wonderful place to get married. So many happy memories here and now, many more. Marianne would be so pleased."

"Aye. She would have been overjoyed." Grace added. "It's heart-warming to see them look so happy."

"A great matchmaking result," Robyn chipped in with a grin. "And I see they're no' the only ones…"

"It appears so," Grace grinned, nodding across at Cedric and Rhona, who were dancing together, laughing happily.

"I think we've finally found him a good, happy match," Maudie said.

"We faced our past," Grace agreed. "Now we can look to the future."

"Aye, we can," Robyn replied. "So who is gonnae be our next match?"

"Wee Dougie needs a partner," Maudie said, remembering the conversation on the minibus over. "But whom to match him with?"

"Leanna is coming to work for me," Grace answered, glancing across at Leanna, who was arm in arm with Joe and then Rory, laughing with delight. "She might be looking for love… I know when I met Paul, I wasn't, but look at us now…"

She watched her husband now as he made his way over from the dance floor, looking decidedly out of puff.

"We were just talking about the night you got engaged," Maudie said, and Paul put his arm around Grace's shoulders, beaming at her.

"I'm so glad you said yes."

"Me too."

· · ·

"We should have a toast. To the future!" Paul announced, raising a glass.

"To the future."

Robyn glanced over at Orion, with a knowing look, and then, almost without thinking, she put her hand on her stomach.

"Robyn?" Grace marvelled, eyes widening. "Are you?"

Robyn nodded, eyes welling up. "We weren't gonnae let anyone know for another few weeks."

"Och, hen, that's the best news! I'm so happy for you!" Grace cried, throwing her arms around her, and felt the tears welling in her eyes. "Your dreams have come true at last!"

"I know!"

"Have you spilled the beans?" Orion asked, as Eilidh and Angus came over.

"What's this?" Eilidh asked, her eyes shining with excitement. "Have you got a secret?"

"Well, it's early days, and we havenae told anyone yet. Orion has gone to let his mother, Aggie know, and I've just told Da, but aye, you're right. We're having a baby."

"Oh my god! That's wonderful!" Eilidh shrieked, flinging her arms around her and bursting into tears. "Are you really? When?"

"Spring."

"Congratulations! Hooray! An anniversary baby!" Eilidh cried, as Angus stepped forward and pulled Robyn into a bear hug.

"Thank you!" Robyn smiled.

"What's the news?" Maudie asked, and then dissolved into delighted sobs when Robyn told her.

"You're gonnae need someone to take over when you're on maternity leave," said Eilidh.

"Aye, but I havnae thought that far yet!" Robyn laughed.

"What about Jo? She's newly qualified," Leanna suggested.

"Aye, she'd be great." Robyn added mischievously. "And I was thinking we could introduce her to Dougie…"

"I was thinking just the same thing!" Maudie exclaimed. "That's who he could make a good match with…"

"What a great idea!" Leanna agreed.

Grace burst out laughing. "It wouldn't be us if they're wasnae any matchmaking, aye?"

"Aye," Robyn said, glancing at Grace with a grin, as they took in Eilidh and Angus, who had were looking at each other as though they were the only ones in the room. "Our last attempt worked out alright, aye?"

"Aye," Grace grinned back, her heart singing with pure happiness. "It definitely did. Come on. Let's dance the night away!"

And taking their hands, dragged them to the dance floor where they did just that.

The following morning, Eilidh stepped into the garden at Honeybee Cottage, holding the wedding garland which Grace had given her, an array of multicoloured roses, and white heather, and a slice of wedding cake.

"Here you go," she murmured with a smile as she placed the cake and garland next to the hive.

"Telling the bees?" Angus asked as he followed her out, and she turned to him, nodding.

"Bringing them up to date on the gossip."

"We'll have to tell them about Robyn's baby soon."

"Aye, we will," she replied, turning to him as he took her in his arms. "And maybe, one day, our own baby..."

Angus's face broke into a grin. "Let's hope so. I cannae wait for us to have a baby."

"A mini beekeeper in the making," Eilidh grinned.

"A mini shepherd."

"They could do both."

"Aye, they could," Eilidh agreed as Angus took her in his arms and kissed her passionately, making her heart sing with happiness.

"I think, before we start planning the baby, we need to plan the honeymoon..."

"Aye, about that..."

Angus's face broke into a grin as he handed her a folded email print out.

Eilidh took it from him, opened it and read it.

"Paris?!" She cried in delight, looking at him in case it was a joke.

"Aye. You've always said you've wanted to go to Paris. What do you think?"

In response she gave a shriek of delight and flung her arms around his neck, kissing him over and over again.

"Thank you! It's gonnae be a wonderful weekend!"

"Well, I was thinking more like a week away..." Angus grinned.

"A week? Can we afford to take that much time away from the farm?"

"I think, after all the hard work we've put into the last few months, we deserve it, Paddington."

She smiled at him, flushing at the nickname he had given her when she had first come back to Mossbrae, when she had worn red wellingtons and a navy raincoat.

"How did you manage to pull this off?" Eilidh giggled, reading the email again.

"With all the wedding planning, it was easy..."

"That's sneaky!" Eilidh teased, grinning at him. "I dinnae know how you managed to keep it a secret!"

"Och, with great difficulty, believe me!"

She burst out laughing, and he admired her now. She really was stunning, he thought, admiring her light brown hair, and bright blue eyes, her cheeks freckled from long summer evenings, making her glow.

Then, he caught sight of her looking, and her cheeks flushed. Angus always had that effect on her, especially in his dark green polo shirt which picked out his eyes.

"You could visit all the tourist places, and eat at the top of the Eiffel Tower."

"Can we do that? Really?" Eilidh asked Angus who nodded.

"Aye. I think so."

Eilidh looked at him with tears of happiness springing to her eyes, and felt her heart surge with happiness and anticipation: A whole week away with Angus, spending much needed quality time together... she suddenly couldn't wait to go.

"Aye. I cannae believe it! I'll have to tell the bees! We're going on honeymoon!"

THE END.

Other Works

I hope you enjoyed reading this book, if you would like to read the other books in the Mossbrae Series, available on Amazon, in Kindle Unlimited and on all good paperback retailers.

A Year at Honeybee Cottage

Christmas at Honeybee Cottage

Keep an eye on for the next book in the Mossbrae series:

Coming Winter 2023

Acknowledgements

Firstly, I would like to thank my family and friends for all their love and support during the time it took writing and publishing this third book. I hope you enjoy reading the final product.

Secondly, I'd like to give a massive thank you to Kirsty, for another brilliant manuscript assessment, which really helps shape the book into something fantastic, and also to Gruff and Angharad at Gwenyn Gruffyd for making such amazing YouTube videos, they have been invaluable when researching for this book.

Love Alexandra.

About The Author

Hello! Thank you so much for picking my book. I hope you enjoy it as much as I enjoyed writing it!

Here's a little bit about me:

I am a full time indie romance author of the contemporary romance series, the Mossbrae series, set in the fictional Scottish village of Mossbrae.

Originally from Yorkshire, I was brought up in a multicultural household (Scottish, British, and Hong Kong Chinese.) I now live in the East Midlands with my husband and two children.

Having always dreamt of being an author, and after a long journey of twenty years, in June 2022, I published my debut novel, A Year at Honeybee Cottage.

I write full time, but when I'm not, I enjoy knitting (toy animals, using Claire Garland's brilliant knitting patterns,) exploring National Trust places with my family on weekends, and binge watching tv boxsets.

Contact me my writer's contacts on:

Twitter @alex_wholey

Instagram @alexwholeywriter

Printed in Great Britain
by Amazon

23690016R00175